SOMEWHERE ELSE

Rodie Sudbery

SOMEWHERE ELSE

ANDRE DEUTSCH

First published 1978 by
André Deutsch Limited
105 Great Russell Street London WC1

Copyright © 1978 by Rodie Sudbery
All rights reserved

Printed in Great Britain by
The Anchor Press Ltd and bound by
Wm Brendon & Son Ltd both of
Tiptree, Essex

British Library Cataloguing in Publication Data

Sudbery, Rodie
Somewhere else.
I. Title
823'.9'1J   PZ7.S9434

ISBN 0-233-96974-8

For Vic and Marilyn

1

'Bruce,' said his mother, 'don't gobble your food like that.'

Bruce slowed down a little. He knew he was eating faster than usual; it was because of the model aeroplane which waited for him upstairs. The delicate job of assembly was finished, and all it needed now was paint. He had planned to do it this morning – Saturday morning, it should have been safe enough, but his mother's demands had left him with barely five minutes to himself. First she had wanted him to dry the breakfast dishes; then he had had to make his bed and tidy his room; and finally there had been the Saturday shopping, which had taken ages as everyone else was doing the same thing and the queues were immense.

He scraped up the last morsel of potato and said: 'Shall I get the pudding?'

'No no, I'll do it, you'll only drop it.' She spoke in the slightly complaining tone which seemed to have become a habit since his father had died. Not that she hadn't used it before; but now it was permanent, at least with him. 'You clear the plates out.'

As he put them beside the sink there was a knock at the back door. He recognised it with gloom; only Mrs Reevy from across the road used that particular rhythm. She was also, probably, the only person who reckoned herself a close enough friend of his mother's to come to the back of the house rather than the front.

'Come in, Mrs Reevy, come in.' There was a note of resigned welcome in Mrs Payne's voice. 'I was just making a cup of tea.'

Lowering her considerable weight into an armchair Mrs Reevy glanced at the table and said, 'There now, I'm interrupting your meal. Just you carry on, dear, don't mind me.'

'Oh, I'd finished,' said Bruce's mother, cutting him a piece of treacle tart. He knew he wasn't expected to follow her example and say he didn't want any; if he'd tried it there would have been sharp words about why did he think she'd gone to the trouble of making it. Anyway, she wasn't going without from politeness. She never did eat much.

Mrs Reevy was sighing over her varicose veins.

'When I think how I used to be!' she lamented. 'Still, after five children what can you expect.'

Bruce tried not to look at her legs, afraid they would put him off his pudding. He was used to his mother's, which weren't so bad. The reason why they were bad at all after only one child was, as he had often heard, that she had had to work in a shop while she was expecting him, on her feet all day during a long hot summer. His father had been unemployed at the time due to one of his bouts of depression. He had suffered from depression off and on throughout Bruce's childhood. In the end, you might say, it had killed him.

'Strange isn't it, that I should have the five all girls, and you just the one boy.'

Bruce ate as fast as he dared, longing to escape. He was totally uninterested in Patricia, Theresa, Deena, Linda and Angela Reevy. Particularly boring were the frequent mentions of Patricia (who had recently married, a good Catholic boy) and Deena (who was the same age as him and supposed to be his friend). He thought of the model upstairs and of the moment when he would dip his brush into the new tin of paint and lay the first shining stroke along one wing.

8

'But you'd almost think it was meant,' (for once Mrs Reevy was skipping the usual details about her daughters) 'when you look at you now, with a grown son to help you and no little ones to worry over.'

Bruce shifted uncomfortably, making his chair creak.

'Such a good boy,' continued Mrs Reevy. 'I saw him this morning loaded down with shopping. I expect he takes a lot of the heavy work off your hands?'

'That depends what it is,' said Mrs Payne wearily. 'Nobody's been near the allotment for months.'

Bruce gave a silent groan. The allotment was a familiar grievance. Under his father's spasmodic care, it had produced a few vegetables from time to time; it was supposed to be good for him to work there, but he had abandoned it some while before his death and nobody had even thought of it until some while afterwards. Then the notion of its wasted resources had begun to bother Mrs Payne. She had tried intermittently to awake in Bruce some sense of responsibility towards it, but had not succeeded. He felt the allotment had never been taken seriously by either of his parents, and he wasn't going to start taking it seriously now.

'Really?' said Mrs Reevy.

'I've been on the point of going down there myself once or twice, but it needs heavy digging and I don't think I could manage that.'

'You'd be mad to try,' said Mrs Reevy warmly. 'You don't want to do your back an injury on top of everything else. But surely Bruce could manage that for you? Why, he'd make short work of it one fine afternoon.'

Bruce said the first thing that came in to his head. 'I don't think we've got a spade.'

'Of course we have,' said his mother, 'it's in the coalshed.'

Mrs Reevy looked at the sunlight streaming through the window. 'Today would be a grand day for it.'

9

'But I was going to – ' He broke off and said instead, hopelessly: 'I'm not sure I know how.'

Mrs Reevy gave a great rolling laugh. 'Heavens above, any healthy boy can dig!'

There was clearly no escape. Filled with despairing rage, he thought the only thing to do was to get it over as quickly as possible. At least he needn't endure any more of Mrs Reevy. It might have looked rude if he'd rushed off so soon to his aeroplane, but as this was their own idea they could hardly object to his departure. He pushed back his chair and made for the door, mumbling, 'I'll get straight round there then.'

'Have you finished your meal?' said his mother.

'Yes thanks.' Couldn't she see his empty dish?

'Don't you want any more?'

'No. Thanks.'

'They're always in such a hurry,' said Mrs Reevy comfortably. 'Goodbye for now, Bruce.'

'Bye.' He turned again to go.

'Bruce,' his mother's voice pursued him, 'if you are thinking of doing any gardening, you'd better wear your old shoes.'

If! He clumped upstairs without replying, feeling he had gained a momentary advantage. She had obviously not expected him to give way so easily.

In the bedroom the sight of the model Lancaster waiting on the chest of drawers renewed his frustration. He kicked off his shoes without untying the laces and left them in the middle of the floor, hoping his mother would see them and be annoyed. Would it have been any use telling her he had other plans for this afternoon? Probably not, considering what those plans were. She had no patience with his hobby; she never had approved of it, right from the first Spitfire bought for him by his father.

He pulled out his old shoes, remembering the excitement

of that moment. It was most unusual for his father to give him a present; and it hadn't even been his birthday. There was a reason for it though. A few days earlier he had been trying to carve a boat out of a block of wood; had failed most dismally, and had in the end, rather timidly, asked his father for assistance. He had been sure his father could help, if only he would; he had often watched in admiration as Mr Payne sharpened one of the pencils he used for drawing, every cut of his penknife going exactly where it was intended, the chips slicing off in a perfect pattern. Mr Payne scorned pencil sharpeners; 'the kind of point you get with them is no use for anything,' he would say, and would sometimes do one of Bruce's pencils too, if in a good mood.

But when it came to the block of wood which was so stubbornly refusing to turn into a boat, he was as helpless as Bruce. 'You're trying something much too difficult,' he said. 'Better give up.' And then, a week later, the little parcel: 'See how you get on with this.'

They had worked on the first models together. ('Wasting time on those fiddly little things,' his mother had said.) Soon, however, Bruce had found he could do them alone; just as well, for his father's continuing interest in a particular topic could never be relied on for any great length of time. He had always liked to see the completed aeroplanes, though. Bruce wished he could see the Lancaster.

If he really got a move on with the digging there should still be time to do some painting afterwards. Thinking this he ran downstairs, and had already dragged the spade from a dark corner of the coalshed when his mother came out to find it for him.

'Perhaps you should wear your old trousers too.' She looked at him uncertainly.

'These are my old trousers.'

'No, I mean your even older ones.'

'Oh, Mum, they hardly come below my knees!' He heaved

the spade over one shoulder and vanished round the corner of the house before she could suggest the Arran sweater that had fitted him when he was ten.

As he went through the gate he saw, across the road, Deena Reevy sitting on her garden wall with a friend. It was like Deena to be posted where she could get a good look at everyone who went by. She wouldn't mind the fact that they could all get an equally good look at her – indeed, she probably enjoyed it. She was wearing a shirt in gaudy stripes, and her black hair was done up in a ridiculous little knot on the top of her head.

'Oh look, there's Bruce!' said her friend.

'Going on the loose,' said Deena, and they both shrieked with laughter. He paid no attention.

'Off to do some digging, are you?' called Deena after him. Immediately he regretted the jaunty angle of the spade, feeling it made him look like a little boy playing soldiers.

'*Don't* answer then!' yelled Deena. 'I suppose it's going to be a grave!' There followed a strangled yelp, and glancing back he saw she had been pushed off the wall by her friend – presumably for being tactless. Under cover of this distraction he lowered the spade to a vertical position just missing the pavement, which soon made his arm ache. When he went round the corner he put it, with some relief, back over his shoulder.

It was quite amazing the way his mother and Mrs Reevy persisted in thinking that he and Deena got on well together. Of course it had once been true; in the days when they were in the same class at St Joseph's they'd been friends, of a rather quarrelsome sort; but that had all ceased two years ago, when they moved on to their secondary schools.

He turned off the road into the recreation ground and followed a path across the middle of the grass, past the swings, and down into a small steep-sided valley. The allotments were at the bottom. He had visited theirs once or twice with his father; he recognised it now partly by the shed in one corner and partly by its air of neglect. It was larger than he remembered, and plentifully covered in weeds; there were also a few rows of straggly dead vegetation which he thought might be last year's peas.

In prospect it was a task to make anyone groan, and before getting started he explored the shed. Not that there was much to explore; it contained nothing but an empty sack and a very old basketwork armchair, unravelling in several places. The chair had been turned out by his mother, years ago; he had had no idea his father had brought it here. Had his mother known? No wonder there had never been many vegetables from the allotment if his father had spent his time down here sitting in the shed. He sat there himself for a moment, looking out through the smeared glass of the window. He felt unpleasantly confined in the small dusty space; he was glad to leave it and start digging.

The work was not without interest. He found occasional potatoes and collected them carefully, thinking his mother ought to be presented with such immediate results from his efforts. There was also, among the weeds, a rather unusual plant – a sort of giant daisy or white sunflower, about three feet tall. The petals were beginning to tarnish, but as he bent over it he caught a strong whiff of its scent and closed his eyes in astonishment, amazed by the jumble of feelings it conjured up. Smells could be powerful reminders, he knew, but of what exactly was this reminding him? There was a confused sense of warmth, and of a safe, right place; and there were words. *Sweet golden clime.* Surely that came from a poem his father had once read to him. About a sunflower? He wasn't sure.

He pulled himself together and lifted the spade once more, but somehow he couldn't bring himself to harm the plant, dying though it obviously was. He dug all round it and left

13

it untouched in its own little island of earth. It looked rather silly, but who was to see?

He had an aching back and blisters by the time the digging was finished. Still, he had done it; now perhaps his mother would be satisfied. He would have liked to leave the spade in the shed instead of dragging it home, but feared he would be sent back to fetch it, as the shed door had no key. Although the armchair had been left untouched all these months a decent spade might well be a different matter.

The potatoes he carried in the old sack. One way and another he was quite out of breath when he reached the top of the steep path leading out of the little valley, and stood for a moment panting. There were children playing by the swings and he noticed with gloom the occupants of the roundabout: Deena and her friend Marian, and a third girl, plump and fair. He rested longer than necessary, dreading the inevitable comments as he walked past. They were using the roundabout as a seat, sprawling at ease and just giving an occasional kick to prevent its coming entirely to rest; they were too absorbed in their conversation to notice that some of the younger children were inclined to object to this mono-poly of the best piece of apparatus.

Deena was declaiming loudly: 'Pat Smith's boy friend is two years older than herself . . . and he lives near the rail-way station . . . and – '

'I deny it, I deny it,' said the girl called Pat, lying back and gazing at the sky with only a faint blush to belie her placidity.

Bruce spotted two boys who went to his school approach-ing from the opposite direction. The girls caught sight of them too, and immediately began to chant the name of a local football team. The boys retaliated with the name of the rival team.

'We shall we shall we shall not be moved,' sang Deena and Marian.

One of the boys sat down on a swing and Deena ran across and joined him, standing astride the seat and insisting that he give her a ride.

'Careful, Deena,' warned Pat lazily, 'he might suddenly turn nasty.'

Marian asked, giggling: 'Are you trying to imitate what you saw that couple doing, Deena?'

'You're too heavy,' complained the boy. She jumped down, grabbed his duffle bag from the grass and ran away, with him in fierce pursuit. Bruce chose this moment to start moving himself. Nobody noticed him as he hurried past the swings; they were too busy watching the chase.

'You've been a long while,' said his mother when he got home.

'It was a long job. Here!'

'Whatever is it?' she said, recoiling slightly from the out-thrust sack.

'Potatoes.'

'*Potatoes?*'

'Yes, from the allotment.' He held the sack open to show the twenty or so earthy prizes lying at the bottom. 'I thought you'd like to have them.'

She looked doubtful. 'I don't suppose they'll be any good *now* – they'll have been too long in the ground. And where on earth did you find that filthy old sack? You'd better put it outside the back door.'

He obeyed in a grumpy silence. But then she asked how much he'd got done, and was impressed when he said he'd finished the job. She suggested that he must be hungry (he was; very) and began to boil eggs for his tea. He went off, whistling, to wash his hands, and viewed with some pleasure the extreme griminess of the water. He decided there was a lot to be said for the exhaustion which followed honest toil.

After his tea, much refreshed, he hurried upstairs to his model. There were no more interruptions. He hummed as he painted the delicate structure, sniffing the clean sharp smell and reminded of the afternoon's other smell – the scent of that strange flower. Not that the two were at all the same. He must look up the sunflower poem; he thought he knew where it would be.

When the first coat was finished he went and searched through the bookcase in the sitting room. He found the volume he wanted; and once he had had the idea of using the index of first lines, he also quite quickly found the poem. He read it to himself, silently, because his mother was in the room.

> Ah Sunflower, weary of time,
> Who countest the steps of the Sun,
> Seeking after that sweet golden clime
> Where the traveller's journey is done:
>
> Where the Youth, pined away with desire,
> And the pale Virgin, shrouded in snow,
> Arise from their graves, and aspire
> Where my Sunflower wishes to go.

He liked it, though it didn't make much sense to him. Indeed on closer examination it seemed to be entirely in the form of a sentence which wasn't a proper sentence at all. Still, he liked the sound of it inside his head.

'What's that you're reading?' asked his mother suddenly, looking up from the evening paper.

'Oh nothing.' He quickly closed the book, feeling an instinctive wish for secrecy.

'What did you say?'

'*Nothing*.' He pushed the volume back into its place, afraid of her sharp eyes.

'Isn't that one of your father's books?' It was as though he had committed a crime.

'What if it is? I can look at them, can't I?'

'Really, Bruce . . .'

He carried on, heedless. '*You* never do.'

After a moment she said remotely: 'I wish you'd try not to sound so rude.'

He subsided into a resentful silence. Really, she did object to the most extraordinary things. No wonder his father had suffered from depression; sometimes Bruce believed he could understand exactly how it had felt. Though he didn't think he would ever follow his father's recipe for escape. An overdose of sleeping pills was too extreme by far.

2

Bruce had supposed his duties towards the allotment would end with the digging, but he soon found his mother had other ideas. She began to talk about home-grown salads; whenever she had to buy carrots and onions she complained afterwards of the poor quality and the high price. Bruce made up his mind that as long as she continued merely to hint, he would pay no attention. Though once, irritated beyond bearing, he did mutter:

'Vegetables aren't *that* easy to grow.'

'What do you know about it?'

'Well Dad never found it all that easy, did he.'

The reference flurried her, as he had hoped it would. 'It's a question of attitude,' she said vaguely, and left it at that.

Then one evening there was a knock at the back door. Not Mrs Reevy's usual knock; Bruce, doing his homework in the next room, heard his mother say: 'Oh hallo, dear. Come in. Bruce! It's Deena!'

He froze.

'Mum thought these might come in handy,' said Deena's voice.

'How kind of her – Bruce! – would you like a cup of tea?'

'No thanks.' (He breathed again.) 'The seeds are some Dad couldn't use.'

Seeds?

'Perhaps orange squash then? – Bruce!'

'No really, Mrs Payne, I must go.'

18

'Well, tell your mother thank you very much, won't you.'

'Yes.' She raised her voice and called cheekily: 'Bye, Bruce!'

He clenched his fists, determined not to answer.

'I expect he's concentrating on some maths. Goodbye then, dear.' The back door closed, and Bruce hunched defensively over his books as his mother burst in from the kitchen, demanding to know what he meant by his rudeness.

'I was busy. And she hadn't come to see me.'

'How do you know what she'd come for?'

'Well, I'm sorry,' he said perfunctorily; then, thinking it would be better to find out the worst without delay: 'What did she bring, anyway?'

'Oh, you're not too busy to take an interest in that?'

'I don't care.' He turned back to his work. 'I expect it was only rubbish.'

'I don't know what's got into you these days, Bruce, you're turning into a very unpleasant person . . .' His mother's voice receded into the kitchen, then returned. 'She brought these.'

It was a typical Reevy present. Two packets of seeds, opened, their tops carefully rolled over; and a small garden hand fork with one of its teeth broken off short. The fork had come from a jumble sale, of course. Bruce was always having to pretend gratitude for one or another of Mrs Reevy's jumble sale acquisitions – sweaters, jackets, even shoes. What was worse, he had to wear them; all objections were overridden by his mother. 'Nonsense, that's lovely cloth, I couldn't afford to buy you anything so good, and the sleeves are only a tiny bit too long, nobody will notice . . .'

He looked more closely at the seeds, hoping to find some reason (like the time of year) for pronouncing them totally unsuitable; but both packets (lettuce and radish) said they could be sown in May, so that was no use.

'We must get them in as soon as possible,' said his mother,

admiring the pictures, 'then we'll be able to have our own salads with cold meals this summer.'

She sounded so cheerful at this prospect that Bruce (who had opened his mouth to remind her of the limp, slug-ridden lettuces which were all his father had ever managed to produce) suddenly felt mean.

'Yes all right. I'll plant them this Saturday,' he said.

'Oh there's a good boy. And if we could get some peas in too . . .'

He frowned at his books, pretending not to hear. Enough was enough.

Setting off for the allotment on Saturday, he thought that at least this time he wouldn't have to carry the spade. The seeds could be stuffed inside his pockets; so could the fork, as soon as he had left the house. And the planting ought not to take very long. He would be home again in an hour, able to make a start on the Messerschmitt he had bought that morning.

As he approached the swings he saw Deena. She seemed to spend half her time there, he thought crossly; did she never have anything better to do? She was sitting on the roundabout while her two younger sisters made it go as fast as they could. Stephen Waddilove was there too, trying to get on, but they weren't giving him a chance. He lived next door to the Paynes, a stolid friendless little boy, apparently fatherless – his mother was so taciturn that nobody knew the truth of the matter, and the favourite theory was that she was really Miss, not Mrs, Waddilove; either that or Mr Waddilove was in prison.

'Diddums waddums, waddy a diddle love then?' taunted nine-year-old Linda Reevy. She was a nasty sharp child, very like her older sister; the teachers at St Joseph's had often called Deena too clever by half.

'Diddums waddums!' echoed six-year-old Angela.

Stephen grabbed at the nearest railing as it went by,

missed, and began to chase it. He was like a panting puppy after its own tail; Deena grinned, and the two younger ones laughed so much they let the roundabout slow right down. At this Stephen forgot about wanting a ride; instead he jumped on them with a bellow of rage, punching all three indiscriminately.

'Don't hit *me*, Stephen,' protested Deena, fending him off, '*I* didn't do anything!'

'Serves you right,' said Bruce under his breath as he went past.

'Pardon?' yelled Deena, but he kept going, plunging with relief down into the valley.

The allotment looked very different from the way it had on his last visit, and he felt quite proud as he saw the rectangle of well-dug brown earth. Though it still compared unfavourably with its neighbours, covered as they were with vegetables in tidy rows. And in fact he found when he got right up to it that the earth wasn't entirely bare; as well as the strange flower he had spared last time (now drooping and dead) there was a rash of tiny new weeds – too small to bother about, he told himself firmly. He decided to plant the lettuces first.

He soon grew irritated with the fork, which was entirely the wrong tool for the job. As fast as he tried to draw out a furrow the sides collapsed and filled it in again. A trowel would have been much better; even the kind of trowel Mrs Reevy might have produced, with a missing handle, or a bite out of its other end.

He got the lettuces finished, straightened up, and saw that the dead plant was right in the middle of where he wanted the radishes to go. As he took hold of it to pull it out, a ripe seed fell from the middle of what had been the flower. They were rather pretty seeds, striped black and yellow and pointed at each end. It suddenly seemed a pity to throw them away, and he collected them carefully in the palm of one hand. He would keep them; in a funny way he felt they would make up for the sack of potatoes, which he had noticed in the dustbin some days after bringing it home. He'd been surprised how hurt the discovery had made him – after all, it wasn't as though his father was around to mind.

He carried the seeds into the shed, thinking he would put them down somewhere until he was ready to go home. Of course he didn't delude himself that his father had planted the strange flower; it was just an unusual weed, but because of the poem there was, for him, a link. He looked at the seeds again. They really were attractive; the contrast between the black and the yellow was so vivid that when he stared hard there was an illusion of movement – the stripes began to shift and shimmer. . . .

And, in the flicker of an eye, his surroundings vanished.

He was in a wood. A wood that was all sound and colour. The sound was made up of birdsong and wind in the branches and a distant extra something; the colour was mostly green, in an astonishing variety of shades – the different trees, the moss on their trunks, the creepers tangled between, the turf underfoot. There were tiny blue and yellow flowers growing in the grass, and quite near was a patch of huge white daisies. The strength of the sunlight could be guessed from the brightness of the colours; even so, because of the sheltering foliage and the fresh breeze he was no more than comfortably warm.

The extra noise was the sea. It was waves breaking on a beach, somewhere to his right. He began to walk that way. As his bare feet pressed the small flowers a faint herbal smell rose and mingled with the spicy resinous scent of the trees. He passed the patch of large daisies and their smell was best of all; familiar and sweet.

He ran, and reached the edge of the wood. Ahead was a wide expanse of grass bordered by rocks, and beyond them the white slope of the beach. Now he was in the full glare of the sun, but he still ran. He stopped for a moment to drag off his only garment, a loose shirt, and left it on a rock; then he rushed down the sand and into the sea.

He swam and floated until he was tired and until the water, which had been pleasantly cool at first, began to feel cold. There was a rock with a flat top near where he had left his shirt and he lay there and dried in the sun. Then he put the shirt on and started wandering along the top of the beach, looking at the ground. The hard white rocks were veined with a different substance, translucent and delicately coloured; chunks of it lay half buried in the sand. He found three good pieces; one pearly, one rose pink, and one a very pale green.

Ahead the trees came to the edge of the beach, and the line of rocks stopped. Here he turned inland and followed a faint path which wound through the wood until it reached a clearing. In the centre of the clearing was the tower.

It was built of pale stone, round, with each floor a room. A passage led in to the foot of the central spiral staircase. Usually he left the doors to the staircase open in the upper floors; the stairs were also lit by tunnels between the floors which ran to the outer walls, where they ended in square windows. The tunnels were made lighter by being lined with the translucent rock. Each window framed a different view, and he paused for a moment by each one. As he went higher he could see over the tops of the trees; there was the beach where he had bathed, and there the grazing grounds of the goats.

The room where he stopped had food on the table, gathered earlier that day. He was hungry. He ate several succulent white roots, a handful of tender green leaf-buds, and two large red juicy fruits. There was also milk in a pitcher, and he took a long drink.

When he had finished he went on up, to a room near the

top of the tower which was full of light. Chunks of the coloured stone lay all about; some untouched, some carved into animals and birds and flowers, or simply into strange, beautiful shapes. He took his knife with the blade of diamond, which cut the stone as though it were the softest wood, and sat down to work. He made a little boat, and when it was finished he looked at it in surprise, and wondered what had put the idea into his fingers; he had no boat of his own.

Suddenly restless, he ran up to the flat top of the tower. The sun was setting and the air had cooled. He could see the goats making their slow way to the tower to be milked. All round the island the miles of empty water moved beneath the sky. It would be evening soon; everything was as it should be.

Bruce opened his eyes and blinked, looking round in a dazed fashion at the inside of the shed. How extraordinary, he must have fallen asleep! He didn't even remember sitting down, and yet here he was in the old chair, and he could tell he had been in it some time, it felt so hard and uncomfortable. His legs were stiff, and the pattern of the basketwork was printed on his wrist; indeed, he felt as though it had printed itself all over him.

He stood up and looked at his watch. Yes, he had slept more than an hour. And the radishes weren't planted yet – he started to hurry outside, then checked himself as something crunched underfoot. Seeds, there were seeds all over the floor. Yes, of course, the ones from the odd plant. He must have fallen asleep with them in his hand.

He gathered them up quickly and put them in a little pile on the single shelf. He was bothered by what had happened; it was almost like fainting or having a fit. But you were supposed to feel dreadful after fainting, weren't you? (And even more so after a fit?) Whereas he was sure he had simply woken from a very pleasant dream. He wished he could remember what it had been about.

He stepped outside, but before he could begin on the radishes he noticed with consternation the figure of Deena Reevy descending the path through the trees. Surely she wasn't coming here – yes, she was.

'Bloody *hell*,' he muttered under his breath.

'Bruce!' she called, while still some way off. He didn't answer until she had got right up to him.

'What do you want?' he said then.

'I've come to see how you're getting on.'

'Oh. Why?'

'There's no law against it,' she said pertly, letting her eyes swing over the allotment. 'Planted the seeds, have you?'

'Of course,' he said.

'I must say you've been down here long enough to plant millions.' She grinned, but he didn't respond. 'Where are they, then? I can't see them.'

'You wouldn't, would you? They're *planted*.'

'Haven't you marked the ends of the rows? How will you know where not to weed?'

'Who says I'll be doing any weeding?' he countered.

'Your mum.'

That was all too likely, overheard by Deena during some conversation with her own mother.

'Mind your own business,' snapped Bruce, angry with the whole pack of interfering females.

'What you do,' continued Deena, ignoring his temper, 'is stick the empty packet on the end of a twig . . . here's one . . .' (she bent down) 'then you can see what you've planted.'

'I know what I've planted,' said Bruce loftily, refusing the proffered twig.

25

'You haven't thrown the packets *away*, have you?'

'No, I – ' He stopped his hand as it moved towards his pocket. Showing her one empty packet wouldn't satisfy her at all; she would ask about the radishes, and guess they hadn't been done. She'd guessed anyway, curse her – guessed that something wasn't right. That was why she was going on about it. Well, he was determined not to give her the satisfaction of having her suspicions confirmed.

' – I'm not using the packets,' he said. 'Stones will do fine. Lettuces –' (he marked them) 'and radishes.'

'And what's *that*?' She pointed to the dead plant.

'Oh, a weed.' Growing right in the middle of the imaginary radishes. Crimsoning, he bent to tug it out, and threw it with unnecessary violence towards the shed.

'Aren't you going to water them?' she said next.

'Water them?' he muttered.

'They won't grow without. Look, there's a tap over there.'

'I've got nothing to carry water in. They'll have to make do with rain.'

'Wouldn't there be a bucket or something in the shed?' She made a determined stride towards it.

'No there would not!' Suddenly furious, he blocked her way. He wasn't letting her see that bare interior, and his father's pathetic chair.

'Well – ' she said, and he noted with astonishment that he had managed to make her quail, 'well, I only thought it might not rain for ages.'

He didn't speak. She half turned, then asked:

'If you've finished, are you coming home?'

'In a minute.'

'You could borrow our watering can if you liked,' she said as she went. He answered with an indeterminate noise.

He couldn't start doing the radishes now, it was too late. And although she seemed to be going, he wouldn't put it past her to come back and catch him at it. He gave her time to get well away; then he followed. His irritation with her filled his mind to such an extent that he never thought of preparing an answer to the question which, inevitably, his mother asked as soon as he got home.

'Where on earth have you been?'

'Down at the allotment,' he said as casually as he could.

'But you've been gone ages. It can't have taken you that long to plant the seeds! You're late for tea.'

'Oh good, is it ready?'

'No, it is not ready. What's the use of getting tea for you if you aren't there to eat it?'

'Well, I'm here now,' he said pacifyingly, 'and I'm quite hungry.'

'You didn't think that *I* might be hungry, did you?'

He didn't say *No, because you never are.* 'Why didn't you have yours without me?' were his actual words.

'And have you come in expecting yours half-way through?'

He escaped to wash his hands, muttering: 'Well it was you who wanted the seeds planted.'

'Of course I did, but it can't possibly have taken this long.'

'Deena was there.' The perfect excuse came to him suddenly. 'We were talking. It held me up.'

'*Bruce.*'

Now what had he done? Somehow he'd made things worse, not better.

'You know that isn't true,' she said. 'I saw Deena half an hour ago and asked if she knew where you were – she didn't think you could possibly still be at the allotment, any more than I did, but she said as she was going down there anyway she'd have a look and hurry you up if you were.'

'She never mentioned hurrying!' said Bruce resentfully.

'So she did find you there just now?'

'Oh – *yes*. Bossy little pest.'

27

'So why invent a story like that?'

'Well, if you must know,' said Bruce, giving up, 'I fell asleep.'

Of course that wasn't the end of it. The discussion lasted right through the meal. Where had he slept, why had he been so tired, how could he sleep in the shed? He was forced to mention the armchair, and that upset his mother more than anything else. She went on and on about it.

'I'd no idea he'd taken it down there. He told me he'd got rid of it. To think it's been there all this while!'

'But what does it matter? It's only an old chair you didn't want.'

'I never said I didn't want it. It would have done very nicely for sitting in the garden . . . many's the time I could just have done with that chair . . .'

It wasn't true, she had wanted it thrown away. She had altered the facts so as to put his father in the wrong. But it was no use arguing; she'd only say he didn't remember properly. He quickly finished his tea and went away to make a start on his model.

As he passed the stairs window he saw Stephen Waddilove at the corresponding window next door. He often sat there when his mother was out, as she was three evenings a week – people had thought what a gay life she led until they noticed the regular hours she kept and decided it must be a part-time job. She certainly didn't look a very gay person; in fact Bruce found her blank stares so unnerving that he usually tried to avoid running into her outside. When she had first come to live here the neighbours had thought she must be foreign, they got so little response to their friendly remarks; later they found she simply didn't like to talk.

Today the familiar sight of Stephen sitting on the stairs triggered in Bruce's mind a rapid shuffle of memories – his father, a poem, a place – a place! Suddenly his dream came flooding back to him, complete in every detail. He went into

28

his bedroom, but he was no longer interested in the new model; all he wanted to do was remember.

He had never dreamed like that before, nothing so vivid or remarkable. It made the lost afternoon seem quite worthwhile. The island was there in his head like somewhere he had really been. Though it wasn't exactly he, himself, who had been there – the boy in the dream was another person, rather like him but not the same; a few years older, for one thing. If only it could be a sort of prophecy. He would like to go back.

Thinking that, he suddenly remembered the very last thing he had done before falling asleep. Of course, he had looked at the seeds; and there had been that funny dazzle effect with the stripes . . .

'It was them,' he said aloud, slowly. 'They must have made me have – well, hallucinations, I suppose.'

He felt relieved that the reason for his strange sleep had been something outside himself. He also felt excited and afraid. Because he would have to try out the seeds again. He knew he would; he couldn't resist it.

3

Mrs Payne usually went to the eight o'clock Mass on Sundays. She was a natural early riser and Bruce wasn't; he was allowed to take himself in a leisurely fashion to the eleven o'clock, while she cooked the lunch. (His father, when alive, mostly hadn't gone at all.)

Afterwards, edging his way through the chatting groups outside, he came face to face with Mrs Reevy.

'Well, and how are you?'

'Fine, thanks,' he mumbled.

'I hear you got those seeds in yesterday for your mother.'

'Yes.' He had a sudden thought. He was going to need an excuse to go back to the allotment today, so why not – 'They need watering though. Deena said you had a watering can I could borrow . . . ?'

'You can, certainly!' Mrs Reevy was delighted. 'I'll send her across with it when we get home.'

'Oh don't bother,' he said hastily, 'I'll come and get it. And thanks.'

Angela ran up and hung on her mother's arm. 'Mum, can we have an ice cream? Linda says – '

'We'll see about that.'

Bruce could see Deena approaching too. He made a hasty escape. If he left now he could avoid their company on the way home; there were bound to be a good few people Mrs Reevy hadn't chatted to yet.

When he reached his own street he decided to go and get

the watering can at once. This would be a good time for it, with the larger and noisier portion of the Reevy family out of the way. Mr Reevy never said much, and Theresa, the oldest now Patricia was married, was the only one Bruce liked. She too had been to early Mass; she opened the door to him with a pen in her hand, and he guessed she was using the quiet morning to study. She wanted to go to university and then teach; Deena often said, disgustedly, that she did nothing but work.

Her eyes focussed on him in vague surprise. 'Oh hallo, Bruce,' she said. Her long dark hair was drawn straight back from her face and tied in a bunch; she had worn it that way for as long as he could remember. Her face, severely beautiful, reminded him of a nun at St Joseph's who had taught him when he was ten. She would be a good teacher, he thought.

'I just came to borrow a watering can,' he said quickly, not wanting to disturb her for longer than necessary.

'Have we got one?'

'Yes, I think so – I mean yes, you have. Your mother said it would be all right.'

'I'll go and see if I can find it. Come in.'

He came as far as the doormat and stood listening to the sounds of her search. Presently she reappeared from the back of the house with the can in her hand. He took it and thanked her; then delayed on the point of hurrying away because of the puzzled expression with which she was looking round the hall. 'You put your pen beside the phone,' he told her.

Her face cleared. 'So I did.'

The rest of the family had just turned into the end of the street as he hurried across to his own house and slammed the door behind him, breathless with relief at their avoidance.

'Bruce!' said his mother.

'Sorry, it slipped.'

31

'What have you got there?'

'I've borrowed it to water the seeds. The earth was very dry when I put them in.'

'Oh, are you going down to the allotment again today?' She sounded quite impressed by his concern. 'Well, you will remember to wear your old shoes, won't you.'

Later, after roast beef and Yorkshire pudding and apple pie, Bruce changed into his old shoes and left the house. It was a fine afternoon; he swung the watering can cheerfully as he walked, pleased to display it as a badge of respectability. When he thought of his real reasons for visiting the allotment he felt a little uneasy, and was glad not to meet any of the Reevys on his way. Perhaps they were still eating their meal.

This was obviously the favourite day of the week for gardening; the allotments were quite well populated when he arrived. One or two people said hallo as he passed, but in the main it was not a talkative occupation – the only human sounds were the chink of tools and the occasional cough.

He got the radishes in first, working with guilty speed. Then he did the watering; he quite enjoyed watching the soil darken under the artificial shower, and pictured the grateful seeds beginning to grow.

He moved casually towards the shed, and put the watering can down beside the door. A quick glance round ensured that nobody was looking in his direction as he slipped inside. There were the striped seeds in a pile on the shelf, exactly as he had left them; he fingered them gently, but didn't look too hard. Remembering their power, he decided it would be best to be sitting down before he tried any experiments. Also, he should arrange if possible not to be holding them in his hand, or he might drop them all over the floor again.

The height of the shelf suggested an idea, and he pushed the chair right up to it. If he sat leaning sideways his face

32

came to the edge of the shelf. Suppose now he put the seeds just *there*, and stared . . .

'We're always coming here,' said Deena.

'S'pose we are,' agreed her friend Marian.

They were sitting one behind the other on the five-seater horse. They were too large for it, and their feet trailed on the ground.

Deena sighed. 'Sunday's so *boring*.'

Stephen Waddilove, unaided, was making the roundabout go. Linda and Angela Reevy were among his passengers. 'Faster, faster!' they shrieked. 'Don't stop yet, Stephen! We're not going fast enough!' His face was scarlet.

'*Oh* oh,' said Marian, straightening up, 'here comes trouble.'

Three boys their own age were approaching over the grass, kicking a football from one to the other.

'Ignore them,' said Deena, turning away with a toss of her head.

'Yes, let's.'

'Oh, Stephen!' cried Angela. 'You shouldn't have stop-ped!'

'I'm sweating,' he panted, flopping against the rails of the roundabout as it carried him round.

'Pooh, are you, Stephen? Don't come near *me*, then.'

'You should say perspire. Animals sweat.'

'Stephen, have you got a French father?'

'Have you got a Chinese father, Stephen?'

'Don't be silly – he'd be *yellow* then. Is he Russian, Stephen? Is your father Russian?'

'Stephen, is your father an Eskimo?'

The shrill voices penetrated the determined abstraction of the older girls. Marian frowned.

'What are they on about?'

'Oh – I think he said at school that his father was foreign

or something. He's in Angela's class.' Deena wasn't interested.

The three footballers made a sudden rush for the swings, on which they began to perform spectacular feats of daring. Meanwhile Stephen gathered all his breath and bellowed: 'NO!' Linda and Angela were momentarily silenced.

One boy took a flying leap from the highest point of the swing.

'Huh,' said Deena. 'I could do that when I was ten.'

Marian arched her back slightly, and asked: 'Do you think this sweater suits me?'

'I could do it *now* if I wasn't wearing these shoes.' She wriggled her feet, loosening them.

'Don't try it,' said Marian lazily. 'You'll ruin your tights.'

'No what, Stephen?' asked Linda. 'No he's not a Russian, or no he's not an Eskimo?'

'Or no he's not a Chinese or a French?'

'Stupid, you don't say a French, it's a Frenchman.'

'Oh well,' said one of the boys, 'I've had enough of this.' He left the swings and began to dribble the ball away.

'Where are you going?' shouted his companions.

'The downs!'

They followed him.

'I must be off too,' said Marian, suddenly brisk.

'Why?'

'Got some homework.'

Deena watched her go, undeceived. Marian fancied sharing a bus ride with the boys; already they were shouting insults at her, and she was cheerfully shouting them back.

The roundabout was slowing down. Stephen jumped, landing clumsily on the concrete surround.

'Oh good, send it fast again!' commanded Angela.

'No. I'm going home.'

Deena's gaze rested idly on his small purposeful figure as it plodded away. Linda and Angela, denied a common victim, began to quarrel with each other. No wonder he was fed up with them, Deena thought; she was too. In fact she was fed up with everything. She stood. On this dull afternoon there was only one occupation that promised any interest at all.

'Where are you going?' asked Linda.

'Mind your own business.' Deena took the path which led down into the valley. It was worth a try; if Bruce was at the allotment she could pass some time happily getting on his nerves.

She wondered for a moment why, of all the boys she knew, Bruce was the one she was most driven to tease. It wasn't as though he ever teased her back; he just grew cross and nasty. She corrected herself – nastier than usual. Perhaps it was because they had once been real friends. She hadn't forgotten it even if he had, and she resented his present aloofness.

She scanned the allotments, the right one easy to pick out because of its bareness. No, he wasn't there, though he obviously had been; she could see the watering can. He must have forgotten it. He might at least have left it inside the shed. Or could he perhaps be inside the shed himself? She quickened her pace as she remembered how determined he had been not to let her enter it the day before.

The door was closed, so she knocked, calling briskly: 'Anyone at home?' She got no reply. Well, now she was here she might as well put the watering can away. She turned the handle, not really expecting anything of interest inside but slightly curious in case there was; and gaped in astonishment at the sight of Bruce, sprawling in an armchair, sound asleep.

It was almost embarrassing for a moment. Then it was funny. The door shut itself behind her with more noise than she intended, but he didn't stir.

'Just look at you snoring away there – you could be inety,' she crowed aloud (unfairly; he wasn't actually snoring.) She continued more to herself: 'And where did you get that awful old chair? That must be what you didn't want me to see yesterday – I suppose you'd been doing the same then, you great dozy lump. Honestly, what a place to sleep!' She glanced scornfully round the shed; bare, expect for the chair, and a pile of funny little black and yellow things on the shelf – seeds, were they? She picked a few up to examine. They were very brightly coloured; in fact they seemed almost fluorescent – the stripes were jumping about in an extraordinary way.

She never felt her legs folding beneath her as she slid quite gently down the wall.

The shape which had appeared on the horizon a few minutes ago was growing fast. It was definitely an island. The girl kept the speedboat pointing steadily towards it, smiling through the spray as it came nearer. She hadn't expected to find an island to explore.

Details began to pick themselves out. Trees, and something showing over their tops – perhaps a tall needle of rock? More important was the shore; cliffs mostly, but directly ahead was a beach. She could land there.

When she was close enough she shut off the engine and let the boat drift, anchoring it a few feet from the sand. The water was so clear she could see straight to the bottom. Rolling up her trousers, she waded ashore.

She was just checking that her knife was in her pocket when the boy appeared, walking quietly over the grass at the back of the beach.

'Hallo!' she called, half disappointed and half glad to have company. He came closer and she went on: 'I'm not the first to find it then.'

'Find what?'

He was staring very hard, she didn't know why. He was

the one who looked odd, wearing nothing but a sort of night-shirt.

'This place – this island,' she said.

'Nobody's ever found it before.' Now he was looking at her boat.

'But you're here.'

'I live here,' he said simply.

She was surprised. 'I thought it looked much too small to be inhabited. I didn't see any buildings. Are there many of you?'

'Only me.'

'Do you mean you live here alone?'

He nodded, and began to ask questions of his own. 'Where are you from? Why have you come?'

'I'm staying with friends on Eldin; I was out in my boat and caught sight of this place, so I decided to come and explore. Can I?'

'I . . . What's Eldin?'

'The big island over there. You can't see it, but that way. How long have you been here?'

'Always.'

Her astonishment grew. 'How do you live? Have you got a house?'

'I have a tower.'

'A tower – oh, that must have been the thing that was higher than the trees!'

'I'll show it to you,' he said abruptly. 'Then I expect you'll want to go. There's nothing else to see here.'

'Well – thanks.' She found his manner rather subduing; but though extraordinary he seemed harmless, she thought. And she certainly wanted to look at the tower.

On the grass beyond the beach goats were grazing. Two white kids bleated and ran towards them, stopping inches away; the boy stroked one and the girl was about to do the same when they skipped off.

'They're very tame,' she said.

'They know me because I milk them – the ones with plenty of milk, that can spare a little. But none of the creatures on the island are timid at all.'

He led her into the wood by a winding path.

'Pretty flowers,' she said. 'I must have some of those – ' She plucked two or three huge white daisies, and then saw his face. 'Do you mind?'

'I . . . suppose not. They'll die now, though.'

'But smell them!' She held them out.

'I know. You can smell them without picking them.'

Dashed, she said nothing else until they entered a clearing and she saw the tower.

'Goodness,' she breathed then. 'Who built it?'

'It's always been there.'

He led her up a spiral staircase to a round room.

'Here.' She handed him the flowers. 'You'd better put these in water if you want them to live a bit longer.'

He poured water from a tall jug into a curious vase of cloudy blue stone.

'I like that,' she said. 'They look good in it.'

'I made it.'

'How?'

'Carved it.' He spoke shortly, as though reluctant to pursue the subject. Or perhaps he just wasn't very used to talking.

'How often do you have visitors?' she asked.

'Never,' he said with chilling satisfaction.

'And don't you ever go anywhere either?' She was half prepared for the answer this time.

'No.'

He took her to the top of the tower and on the way she caught glimpses of other rooms through half open doors. They seemed either bare or, like the one he had showed her, furnished sparsely. When they came out on to the flat roof she ran to the parapet.

'You can see all over the island.'

'Yes.'

'It's quite small, isn't it? Oh, there's my boat! That means Eldin must be – let me see – roughly over there. You can't see any sign of it even from up here.' But she guessed from his face that he didn't want to hear about Eldin. 'You could have watched my boat coming. Did you?'

'No, I was in the wood. I heard it. It was very loud.'

'Yes, it has a powerful engine.' He didn't want to hear about that either. She spun in a slow circle, her eyes following the horizon. 'No land at all,' she murmured. 'Do you ever feel lonely?'

'No. Never.'

Again that satisfaction. This time it had its effect.

'Well, I'd better go I suppose. Thank you for showing me what you did.'

'There's very little to show.'

He walked back to the boat with her, and on the way she exclaimed in sudden rebellion: 'But I haven't really explored.'

He didn't speak.

'Maybe I'll come again another day.'

After a moment he said: 'Maybe it's so small you won't be able to find it again.'

'We'll see.'

When she had started the engine and headed the boat out to sea she turned and waved, but he didn't notice; his back was turned and he was already walking away.

Deena woke and found herself on the floor of the shed, right next to the armchair in which Bruce was sprawled. Covered in confusion she edged away and scrambled to her feet. Bruce was still sleeping, but she had lost all desire to jeer at him because of it; she only wished to escape. Something had happened to her, and until she understood what she didn't want anyone to know about it, particularly Bruce.

She slid softly to the door and put her hand out to open it. As it moved the hinges gave a loud squeak; Bruce's eyes flew open, and she was caught.

'Oh bother,' she said wildly, 'I didn't mean to wake you.'

'No, I . . .' Not as quick to surface as she had been, Bruce rubbed his face and yawned. 'It's all right,' he began again, slightly hoarse, 'I wasn't really sleeping.'

'I see.' But obviously she didn't put enough conviction into her voice, because Bruce said suspiciously, 'Have you only just come?'

'Yes! I – ' (now what had she done with it? Oh, there it was) ' – was putting our watering can away, I mean I thought you'd left it behind; I didn't know you were in here.'

'I just sat down for a minute.'

'Lucky you had somewhere to sit,' she said without quite meaning to; and quickly averted her eyes from the floor in case he should guess that her seat had been there.

He stood up. 'I got the watering done.'

'Yes, I noticed.'

'You can take the watering can if you want.'

'Ooh can I really, sir, thanks, and shall I hold the door for you too?' She was glad to hear her usual mocking tone return, instead of the unnatural politeness due to embarrassment.

'Oh I'll take it.' He snatched at it as he went through the door she ceremonially held. She realised it was going to be difficult now to avoid a joint walk home, and she really didn't want his company.

'I expect you've got other jobs still to do,' she suggested, looking at the plot of earth.

'No,' he said as though answering an accusation. 'Everything's done.'

'Race you to the swings then!' she said, and ran, thinking it would be easy; but he passed her half-way up the slope and reached the swings well ahead.

'You never used to be able to run like that,' she said indignantly. If she'd been first, she hadn't intended to stop.

'My legs have grown,' said Bruce. 'I'm taller than my mother now.'

'You're certainly taller than me.' She glanced sideways as they walked on together.

'Yes,' Bruce agreed.

'Your father was quite tall, wasn't he.'

He grunted.

'Do you talk about him much – you and your mum?'

'Yes – no – well, I mean, I suppose so, yes.'

'What *do* you mean?' asked Deena curiously.

'I don't know!' He sounded so irritable she said no more.

They left the recreation ground and presently came to their own street.

'Going to deliver the watering can yourself?' asked Deena with a grin.

'Oh – no, you can take it. That is – ' he corrected himself meticulously, 'would you mind taking it, please?'

'Not at all.'

She couldn't blame him for wanting to avoid her house, she thought when she entered a minute later and found the radio and television both on, Linda quarrelling with Angela, Theresa reading with a frown and her fingers in her ears, and Mrs Reevy in full flood in the kitchen.

'Gracious, Deena, wherever have you been, the younger ones got back ages ago – and don't dump that watering can there, you know where it goes, out at the back – has Bruce finished with it then?'

'Yes. I've been with him down at the allotment.'

'I see, well Marian phoned and she wants you to go round after tea but I said I didn't know – have you done all your

41

homework? – and when did you change into those filthy jeans, I told you not to wear them any more until they'd been washed – where are you going?'

'To put the watering can away!'

Oh to be Bruce, thought Deena for a moment outside the back door. Usually she liked her noisy home, and valued the fact that she was allowed to make quite a lot of noise herself; but just now she felt she would have given anything for a bit of peace to sit and think.

4

A couple of days later instead of coming straight home from school Bruce, on a sudden impulse, took a bus to the cemetery. He didn't quite know why he was doing it, but when he arrived he was glad to be there. His father had been in and out of his head more than usual since the weekend, and somehow in visiting his grave he felt he was affirming his right to think about him if he chose. After the tragedy of his death (politely called an accident, though nobody believed that really) Bruce had felt that well-meaning friends and relatives were, without quite saying so, urging him and his mother to forget. Brooding was bad, the whole sad business was over now, they must think of the future – but Bruce wanted sometimes to remember the past.

It was the dreams that had put his father into his head, the second even more than the first. He felt that if he had to dream another person on to his island, it should have been his father, not some strange girl. Not that she had been quite strange; he had realised, some time after waking, that she had borne a slight but definite resemblance to Deena Reevy. No fact could have annoyed him more. He knew it was totally unreasonable to blame Deena, but he blamed her all the same – not content with haunting him at the allotment, must she even intrude into his dreams?

It would have made sense for his father to be there. The island was connected with him through the white flowers and the poem. He would fit in there; a traveller whose journey was done. Bruce found the idea of Heaven very vague

43

and uncomforting, on the whole (Hell was worse of course, if one could believe in it – Bruce couldn't quite) but the island was different; it was easy to imagine his father there, happy. Why couldn't he have dreamed that?

An old woman glanced at him as she passed and he felt embarrassed, seeing himself as he must appear to her, a pathetic figure with his hands in his pockets and his head bowed with grief. He was glad she couldn't know that he was suffering such a particular childish regret. As though it mattered, really, what happened in a dream – however extraordinary and special the dream might be. Anyway, he must go; it would be a lot later than usual by the time he got home, and his mother would want to know why.

He had been lucky on Sunday; after saying goodbye to Deena he had entered the house and found his mother with her feet up, lost in the rare indulgence of an afternoon nap. He had woken her with a cup of tea, and she had never known how long he'd been away at the allotment.

It was no use hoping for such good fortune today. He slunk quietly through the back door and waited for the eruption.

'Bruce, wherever have you been? Do you know you're nearly an hour late?'

'I'm sorry. I didn't think it was that much.'

'I've been worried about you. You weren't kept in, were you?'

'No – they don't do that at school.'

'Well, did you miss the bus? But you'd have had to miss more than one!'

Bruce said quickly: 'I went to the cemetery.'

'The cemetery!'

He looked down, fiddling with the strap of his bag. He knew his mother didn't like it, but she couldn't say so outright; she would have to find some reasonable objection. Which she did.

44

'Why on earth didn't you tell me that's what you were going to do? You might have known I'd worry. You could have told me this morning.'

'I didn't know then. I just felt like it all of a sudden.'

'Well really, Bruce, you're not a baby. You can't rush off doing things just because you feel like it all of a sudden.'

'No,' he said dejectedly. 'I suppose not.' For one thing it wasn't worth it if there was to be all this fuss afterwards.

'And you knew I was going out this evening. Or had you forgotten?'

'I had actually.' Mrs Reevy had persuaded his mother to accompany her to a coffee evening at the church hall. 'But you're not going for ages yet, are you? I can't have made you late for that.'

'It's no help having my routine upset,' replied his mother, refusing to concede a single point. He apologised again and she said no more. He felt, illogically, that the subject of the cemetery had been left in mid-air; she should have had some questions to ask, but what? One couldn't enquire how the grave had been looking.

It seemed he had made her think about his father, though; and her thoughts took a most unwelcome turn. As they were eating their tea she suddenly remarked: 'That old chair down at the allotment – you might as well bring it back here.'

'*Here?*'

'Yes, I'd like to have it now it's turned up. It would be very handy in the garden.'

'But we don't need it, do we? We've got deckchairs. It's not worth dragging all this way.'

'If it was worth dragging down there I suppose it's worth dragging back,' she said sharply.

'It's so old it'll probably drop to bits if I try to move it.'

'It didn't drop to bits when you sat in it, did it?'

The reference to his sleeping made him feel awkward.

'Anyway I'd like you to see to it sometime.'

45

He muttered something noncommittal, hoping she would forget. Apart from finding it useful he liked having the chair in the shed for its own sake; by now he felt it belonged there.

After Mrs Payne had washed the tea things with Bruce drying, she left for the church hall. He said goodbye cheerfully, looking forward to an evening alone. He didn't intend to make any spectacular use of his freedom, but it would be pleasant to do his homework lolling in an armchair by the fire instead of sitting at the table, and he'd be able to break off for coffee and biscuits whenever he felt like it.

Half an hour later he put the kettle on and went up to his room for a magazine about model aeroplanes which had been lent him by a boy at school. Stephen Waddilove was in his customary perch on the stairs. Something about the small, still figure was different from usual; Bruce stopped on his way down for a second look. Then he looked again. It was difficult to be sure, because instead of facing the window Stephen was gazing straight forward; but – yes – he was crying. Bruce could see the tears rolling down his cheeks.

His first instinct was to duck out of sight. If it had been himself he wouldn't have wanted anyone to know. Then he remembered that Stephen was only six; too young to mind who knew, and probably young enough to hope somebody would do something about it. Because it was one of Mrs Waddilove's evenings out, of course. So it was up to Bruce.

Gripped by awful indecision, he wished desperately that his mother was there. Or even Mrs Reevy – he would rather have appealed to her, if she'd been in, than venture next-door alone. He had another quick look through the window. Stephen was still crying.

He thought with sudden relief of Theresa. She would be able to deal with the situation, he was sure; her calm face and quiet manner would be just what was needed. He would go and ask her at once. There was no danger of running into Deena; he knew she was round at Marian's, having heard

46

her shout this intention down the length of the street earlier on.

He had a last glance at Stephen to see how to describe him (not yelling or anything, but floods of tears) and hurried out of the house.

Deena sat in front of the television, half her attention on the programme and the rest elsewhere. The house was unusually peaceful for once. Both her parents were out; the two younger ones were in bed (Angela asleep, and Linda keeping very quiet in case anyone remembered her and told her to stop reading); and Theresa was doing her homework in the next room. Deena should have been doing homework too (that had been her excuse when she rang Marian to say she wouldn't be coming round after all) but she didn't feel like it. It hadn't been her real reason for not wanting to go to Marian's, anyway. She wasn't sure what had. Perhaps she had just wished to be alone to think about the strange happenings of Sunday. That was certainly what she was doing.

Of course, the key to it all was those seeds. She had stared at them and they had sent her to sleep; or had it been a kind of trance? Anyway, the same thing must have happened to Bruce. She guessed it had not been the first time for him, or he wouldn't have been so nicely settled in the chair, with the seeds in such a handy pile on the shelf beside his head. Did he do it because he liked the dreams he got? She could understand that if his dreams had been anything like hers. She remembered how it had felt, speeding over the sea and landing on the island – only the island had been rather spoiled by the boy who lived on it. 'If I'd been me in the dream and not that girl,' she said to herself, 'I'd have been a lot ruder; the way I am to Bruce. Come to think of it he was rather *like* Bruce.'

She thought about Bruce. She was very glad she'd been the first to wake. It wasn't so much that she minded him

47

knowing she'd touched his precious seeds – she could brazen that out if she had to – but she wouldn't have liked him to see her, as she had seen him, locked in helpless sleep. On the floor, too. At least if she ever tried the seeds again she would know what to expect.

She had to admit that she was quite interested in trying them again. Since Sunday the allotment fascinated her; she had actually paid it a quick visit the evening before, going not with any very clear intentions but just (she had told herself) to see whether Bruce was there. There had been no sign of him; she had glanced through the shed window and seen that it was empty, and also that the seeds were on the shelf. She might have gone inside but for an old man digging nearby – he'd been facing her way and she hadn't quite had the nerve.

Theresa came through, glancing at the screen as she passed.

'Is that any good?'

'Not much,' said Deena.

'Why watch it then?' But she didn't seem to expect an answer. 'Would you like some coffee?' she called from the kitchen.

'Yes please.'

'Oh by the way, can you remind me to tell Mum Bruce has borrowed the watering can?'

'What?' said Deena, suddenly alert. 'When?' *Scrub the coffee*, she nearly added, *I feel like a walk.*

'Oh . . . Sunday, I think it was.'

'That's *history*,' groaned Deena, subsiding.

'Mm?' She was rattling spoons and mugs about.

'He brought it back Sunday as well.'

'Oh did he? How efficient. I suppose he's always been like that though – a careful kind of boy.'

Deena said snappishly: 'He jolly well hasn't always been such a dreary old wet.'

48

Theresa came and leaned in the doorway with a face of mild surprise. 'I thought you liked him.'

'You sound like Mum. Why isn't anyone in this family up to date on my life?'

'Because it's so changeable?' suggested Theresa.

'I'd rather be changeable than stuck, like you.'

Theresa turned away to attend to the kettle, not offended by this remark; Deena had known she wouldn't be. She liked being the kind of person she was.

Taking her coffee, Deena said: 'Can you imagine Bruce ever doing anything a bit adventurous?'

'What kind of thing?'

'Oh . . . getting himself hypnotised. Or taking drugs. Or driving a speedboat or living on an island,' she ran on, her sister's serious expression making her frivolous.

'I think he's too sensible,' said Theresa slowly. 'You wouldn't try it, would you, Dee?'

'A speedboat? Just give me the chance!'

'I meant drugs.'

'Oh, we-e-ell . . . why don't you sit down with that?' she said, irritated by the way Theresa was hovering and sipping from her mug.

'I was going to have it in other room.' Theresa perched temporarily on the arm of a chair.

'What was the stuff people took for dreams? Opium?'

'*In Xanadu did Kubla Khan* . . . but it wouldn't just be dreams. You'd do yourself permanent damage.'

Deena laughed. 'Don't look so worried, I'm not likely to get the chance of it any more than a speedboat.'

Theresa smiled reluctantly.

'And don't tell Mum.'

The smile vanished. 'Why – *were* you serious really?'

'Of course not. That's *why*.' The doorbell rang, a welcome interruption. 'Now who – oh, maybe it's Marian.'

But it was Bruce. Slightly taken aback to see the person

they had just been discussing, Deena said the first thing that came into her head. 'Hallo, do you want to borrow a spade?'

'We've got one.' Bruce looked more than slightly taken aback to see her, she thought. Silly; who did he expect?

'Oh yes, of course. Well – what, then?'

'I don't want to borrow anything, it's just . . . I know your mother isn't here; I thought Theresa would be, though.'

Deena stared. 'She is.' Why on earth was he blushing?

'Oh – well, it's Stephen. He's crying. I saw him through the window and he's been doing it for quite a while. Only his mother's out, and I don't quite know – '

'I'll come,' said Deena promptly, welcoming the little drama. 'Theresa's working, as usual,' she added as she closed the door behind herself. *And even if she wasn't she'd diddle about and be no use at all.*

'Thanks,' said Bruce without much conviction.

They crossed the street. 'Which window?' asked Deena, surveying the front of the Waddiloves' house.

'Stairs, but I don't think you can see him unless you're in our house looking across. I suppose we'd better check he's still doing it, hadn't we.'

Inside the house clouds of steam were issuing from the kitchen. 'Something's boiling,' said Deena; she went to investigate, and switched off the gas under a madly rattling kettle.

'I forgot it,' said Bruce.

She picked it up and shook it. 'Boiled dry, just about. Lucky I came. Theresa would never have noticed.'

'*I* would though,' said Bruce rather sharply.

'Never mind anyway, let's go and look at Stephen.'

She didn't expect there would be anything to see – the stairs, after all, not a very likely place – but there he was sure enough, a picture of silent misery.

'He often sits there, but I haven't noticed him crying before.'

'Have you tried shouting?' Deena flung open the window and leaned out. 'Stephen! Hey, Stephen!'

'No, wait – I don't think – ' Bruce sounded alarmed. Probably his mother would never dream of shouting from house to house. Nor would Mrs Waddilove, come to that.

Stephen was looking in their direction with a startled face.

'We're coming across!' yelled Deena, and with exaggerated patience to Bruce: 'It's all right, I don't intend to jump.'

The back door was locked when they tried it, so they went and knocked at the front. 'This'll be easier for him to open,' said Deena. 'I suppose his mother really is out?' She laughed at Bruce's horrified expression. 'She will be, she always is on Wednesdays.'

They heard slow footsteps inside, and Deena called through the letterbox. 'Stephen, it's us. Can you turn the knob and let us in? Do you know how?'

Nothing happened for a few seconds. Then the lock squeaked and the door began to open. Stephen peered out.

'It's all right, it's only Bruce and me,' said Deena, firmly pushing her way into the house. Stephen looked at her with doubt, wiping his eyes on his sleeve and sniffing. 'Come in and shut the door,' she said over her shoulder to Bruce, who was hovering on the step. 'He'll catch his death in nothing but pyjamas.'

Bruce obeyed.

'Now then, what's the trouble? Why aren't you in bed? Did you have a bad dream?'

Stephen sniffed.

'Do you want your mother?' asked Bruce.

'What's the use of saying that when he can't have her,' snapped Deena in an undertone. To Stephen she continued: 'Are you feeling ill? Have you got a pain in your tummy or anything?'

He shook his head. He obviously didn't want to say why

51

he'd been crying, and Deena decided it didn't much matter, now that he'd stopped.

'I think you ought to be in bed, you know,' she said. 'It's quite late. Linda and Angela are in bed, and Angela's been asleep ages. You look cold, too. Haven't you got any slippers?'

'They're lost,' said Stephen hoarsely.

'His toes are blue,' Deena muttered to Bruce; then, louder: 'Come on, show me where you sleep and I'll tuck you in.'

'And I'll tell you a poem,' said Bruce, surprising her.

Apparently stunned by all this kindness, Stephen turned and trailed upstairs. His room was too bare to be untidy, but the bed was a wild tangle of blankets and sheets. Deena was relieved to find it dry; the sight of it had briefly suggested a new reason for Stephen's recent distress. She dragged at the covers until they were approximately straight, turned back one corner and said: 'Hop in. Do you need the toilet first?'

'No.' Stephen climbed into bed and sat looking at Bruce.

'He wants his poem,' said Deena, and swallowed a grin as she waited to see what it would be.

'Lie down then,' said Bruce. 'It's one that's just right for you.' He waited until Stephen's head was on the pillow and then began:

> Halfway down the stairs is a stair where I always sit.
> There isn't any other stair quite like it.
> It isn't at the bottom; it isn't at the top
> But that is the stair where I always stop.
> And –

His voice faltered. He's forgotten it, thought Deena. He was silent for a moment and then finished in a rush.

> And I often sit there when I ought to be in bed,
> It isn't really anywhere, it's somewhere else instead.

52

Stephen seemed perfectly content with this performance, so Deena bent and tucked him in, saying: 'There, you're all right now, aren't you? You be a good boy and go to sleep, and we'll stay for a little downstairs. Goodnight.'

'Night,' said Stephen.

As they descended the stairs Deena said with a grin: 'That was fudged together a bit, wasn't it?'

'Well, the last line was right,' said Bruce, 'and I think the first four were, but I forgot the middle.'

'He liked it anyway. And it was quicker than a story.'

'It's one my father used to read to me.'

'Did he often read to you?' said Deena curiously. Mr Payne had never seemed to her the kind of parent to take much interest in children.

'No, hardly ever. That's why I remember the times he did.'

'I say, why were you so funny the other day when I asked if you and your mother talk about him much?'

As soon as the words were out of her mouth she regretted them; they'd be bound to spoil this moment of unusual friendliness.

But no; Bruce was answering properly, only pausing to find the right words. 'Well I suppose . . . the thing is, when we do talk about him it's always in a narking kind of way – like there's that chair, the one in the shed; when I said it was there she got terribly cross because he'd taken it down there without telling her, although it's only an old one, and I'm sure she'd thrown it out anyway – but now she says I'm to bring it back so she can use it in the garden, but I don't think she really wants it, it's just – sort of – getting even with him. I just wish,' he finished with a sigh, 'we could sometimes remember him with love – that's all.'

His indignation about the chair had made him quite red in the face. Deena could sympathise; she had often thought

53

that as mothers went Mrs Payne would be a worse trial than her own.

'Can't you keep putting it off?' she suggested. 'I don't suppose she'll go down there and fetch it herself, will she?'

'No. I'm hoping that'll work.'

He wouldn't be able to dream so comfortably without it, of course. Deena's heart gave a little jump as it occurred to her that this would be a good moment to bring up the subject of the seeds.

'I wonder,' she said circuitously, 'if Stephen *had* had a bad dream?'

'I don't think he'd been to sleep at all.'

'Do you dream much?'

'A normal amount, I suppose.' He sounded rather stiff.

'I had a terrific one the other day . . . – what are your best dreams like, are they very vivid?'

'They're all right.'

It was no use; he had turned right back into the prig she found so unbearable. 'Oh keep your old dreams then,' she said, turning away, 'I suppose they're too shocking to repeat. I'm going to look at Stephen.'

He didn't accompany her. Stephen's eyes were closed and he was breathing deeply; he was either asleep or on the verge of it. She returned to the hall.

'It's all right. We can go.'

'Are you sure?'

'See for yourself if you don't believe me. Or you can always sit halfway up your stairs keeping watch.' She held the door open. 'Go on, I'll shut it, you might let it slam.'

He walked through looking very huffy, obviously all set to return to his own house without a word.

'Do let us know if there are any further problems,' she said sweetly. 'Next time you can have Theresa.'

She was glad to see she had dented his composure.

'Thanks,' he muttered, and fled.

5

The following afternoon Deena sat on the garden wall, putting the greatest distance possible between herself and her mother, whom she suspected of wanting her for various boring jobs. Linda and Angela were riding bicycles up and down the pavement with some of their friends. Stephen Waddilove, bikeless, was giving rides to a three-year-old on her small horse with wheels.

'Mind out, Stephen,' said the others. 'You're in the *way*.'

'Deena!' called the voice of Mrs Reevy, faintly. Deena swung her legs and paid no attention. She looked critically at the shadow of her head on the ground and wondered if the two bunches into which she had divided her hair were symmetrical.

'Let me have a go of your bike,' Stephen begged everyone, but they wouldn't.

'Ask your Dad to send you one from China,' said Linda.

Deena thought of foreign countries, and of strange seas dotted with uncharted islands. Why hadn't she been more direct with Bruce the evening before? She should have mentioned the seeds.

Stephen had changed places with the three-year-old; she was trying to push him now, but the horse sagged under his weight and refused to move.

'Get off that, it's Julie's!' said her brother. 'It's for little kids, not big fatties like you – you'll break it.'

Mrs Reevy appeared at the front door. 'Oh, *there* you are.

Didn't you hear me calling? Come and tidy your half of the bedroom, will you? The floor's covered in clothes and I shan't have time tomorrow to sort out which need washing.'

'Yes, I'll do it,' said Deena, not moving.

'When? I don't want to have to keep on telling you.'

'I'll do it later. I can't now; Marian'll be here at any moment.'

'Well you mind you don't forget.' Still grumbling to herself, she went back inside.

Stephen came slowly up to the wall and stood looking at Deena's feet. She lifted one and gave him a gentle prod in the chest.

'Sleep all right last night?' she said.

He nodded.

'No more crying?'

He shook his head.

'What did your mother say about us coming in?'

'Didn't tell her.'

Deena grinned. 'You've got more sense than I thought.'

Stephen smiled back uncertainly, but just then Deena's attention was distracted by Bruce, emerging from his house opposite. She waved so that he would notice her talking to Stephen; she was sure he too would want to check that all had been well last night. He would probably be very relieved to hear that Mrs Waddilove hadn't been told of their intrusion.

Bruce ignored her wave; he kept to his own side and started to walk away. 'Hey!' said Deena indignantly. He turned his head, and she was stuck; nothing she wanted to say could be shouted across the street. 'Hey, where are you off to in such a hurry?' she managed.

'Nowhere,' he said, and went on, leaving her fuming. Nowhere indeed! He was going to the allotment, she was sure of it. Couldn't wait to get there either, by the look of him. Off for another seedy dream – she repeated the last two words inside her head; their disreputable sound made her grin to herself, but she was not pleased, when she looked down, to catch an answering grin on Stephen's face.

'What are you smirking at?' she asked him.

'I – ' he said, 'I – '

She jumped off the wall.

'I didn't tell my mother,' he said.

'I know.' She brushed him aside with one hand.

'Where are you going?' he asked, getting in front of her again.

'Nowhere.' Unconsciously she echoed Bruce.

'Can I come?'

'No, of course not,' she said, with a glare fierce enough to put off the most determined follower.

'I thought you were watching for Marian?' Linda called after her as she escaped.

'I've changed my mind!'

'What shall I tell her if she comes?'

'Oh – say I got fed up waiting.'

Silly, she thought a moment later; Linda would make a meal out of it and the result might be a quarrel. Though Marian probably wouldn't turn up anyway; lately they hadn't been getting on as well as usual, and Marian had only half said she might come.

Deena increased her pace a little. Marian, if she did come, might look for her at the swings; but she wasn't very likely to try the allotments.

Bruce, walking fast, was glad he'd put Deena in her place so firmly. She was a great deal too inquisitive, like all females (except Theresa Reevy, he amended). Look at her last night asking Stephen all those questions about what was wrong, instead of giving him a bit of comfort to make him feel better. And then she'd somehow managed to get Bruce talking about his parents in a way he'd instantly regretted. No wonder he'd blushed; he almost blushed now, recalling a particularly gooey remark about remembering his father with love.

He had told his mother he was going to see if the allotment needed weeding, and when he arrived he did glance round at the weeds for just long enough to check that they were still too small to bother with. Then he ducked inside the shed. The seeds were piled on the shelf. He meant to take them with him when he left; they were too precious to lie around here.

As he sat in the chair and leaned towards them he tried hard to clear all thoughts of Deena out of his head. He didn't want the girl who looked like her intruding into his dream today.

He was in his workroom high in the tower. He stood by one window holding a small cube made of six interlocking pieces in different shades of pearl. He had just finished carving the last piece. He took it apart and put it together again; it was easy for him, but would be a puzzle to anyone else. Though of course no one else was going to try it. There *was* no one to try it.

He put it in his pocket and went towards the stairs. He was hungry. He didn't eat at once, however; instead he went to the top of the tower. He had been up here more than usual in the last few days. He came to look at the sea. His eyes circled the horizon, dwelling longest in the direction in which the girl had told him the island of Eldin lay. He seemed to be continually and anxiously impelled to check that he could see no sign of it. He wished he had never heard of its existence.

Suddenly his gaze shifted closer. There was something on the sea. A moving dot, coming straight for the island. It was that girl again!

He went slowly down the stairs, left the tower and walked

58

through the wood. She came to the same beach as before; he was in time to see her wading ashore.

'I found my way back,' she said.

'Yes.'

'You don't sound surprised.'

'I saw you coming, just now.' He added, surprising himself: 'But I think I was expecting you anyway. Some time.'

'And here I am. Do you suppose my boat is safe there?'

'I expect so. I don't know much about boats.'

'Haven't you got one yourself?'

'No.'

'Of course, you never leave the island.' She smiled suddenly. 'How about coming for a ride in mine?'

'No – no, I don't think so. I have to eat.'

'That sounds a good idea.' She was still smiling.

He asked reluctantly: 'Would you like to eat with me?'

'Yes. Thank you. I would.'

As they walked through the trees she looked about her and said, as though giving herself an instruction: 'Don't pick the flowers.'

'I never do.' He remembered he had told her that before.

'I'm surprised you milk the goats.'

'I only take what I need, and only from the ones with plenty to spare.'

When they reached the tower she glanced at one of the other paths leaving the clearing and said: 'I'd like to explore that way today.'

'All right,' he said. She obviously wouldn't be satisfied until she'd seen all over the island.

In the room where he usually ate he found mugs and plates for them both and laid out the food.

'Don't you ever have anything cooked?' she asked.

'Hardly ever. Those are good,' he said, pointing to some knobbly yellow roots. She took one and nibbled it cautiously.

'Yes, they are.' She sounded agreeably surprised. After

that she tried most of the other things, and ate nearly as much as him. She refused milk, asking what else there was to drink.

'Only water.'

'Then I'd better have water.' He poured her some. 'Is there a spring on the island?'

'Yes.'

'Lucky.' She looked round the room and noticed the oil lamp on a shelf. 'You have light at night, then?'

'Of course.'

'How do you manage for supplies of oil, if nobody ever comes here?'

'Everything I need is in the storeroom at the bottom of the tower.'

'For *ever*?' she said disbelievingly. 'Who put it all there?'

He didn't like her questions. He put his hand in his pocket and fingered his carved cube for comfort.

'How long have you been here?'

'I've never been anywhere else.' He pulled out the cube and began to take it apart. She watched, her attention caught. 'There,' he said. 'See if you can put it together again.'

She fingered the pieces. 'Did you make it?' He nodded. 'It's beautiful. Do you do much of this? Where do you get the stone?'

'There's plenty on the island.'

She puzzled over the cube for quite a while, and then asked him to help her.

'It's good,' she said. 'Can I see some of the other things you've done?'

He felt just as he had when she'd been there before; he didn't want to take her into his workroom. 'I'll fetch one,' he said.

He chose the little boat. 'I made this a few days before you came the first time,' he told her.

'Did you? How strange!' She played with it for some minutes, seeming reluctant to put it down.

'I expect you'd like to explore now,' he said, holding out his hand for it.

'I wish you'd make me one.' She gave it back. 'Yes, let's explore.'

She had wanted him to give her that one, he thought as he led the way down the spiral staircase. But he couldn't; he didn't fancy the idea of her carrying any part of him away with her when she left the island.

He took her to the spring. They both drank a little from it in cupped hands, where it bubbled out of the ground near the top of a slight hill. Then they followed it down to the sea and walked along the shore. They reached the rocky beach where the coloured stones were found, and although he didn't mention them she spotted a small piece of deep blue in the sand, and pounced on it.

'Oh look, that's pretty!'

'Yes,' he said guardedly. He was wishing he'd seen it first; it was a long while since he'd had any quite that colour.

She looked sideways at him, and said: 'I am allowed to collect pebbles, I suppose? It's not like picking flowers?'

'No – but if you take them I can't use them.' He knew it sounded grudging, but he didn't care. And it wasn't his only reason for wanting her to leave the coloured stones alone: he feared that if she took them away and showed them to other people they might all want to come to the island getting the precious stuff for themselves.

'There's another!' She picked up a yellow one. 'Do you really need all that's here?'

'I'd rather you didn't take any.' She was darting ahead and seemed not to hear, bending now and then to the sand. Perhaps she had only returned to the island to see if it had anything worth taking. He stood helplessly watching her avaricious progress, picturing a crowd of people all doing the same; maybe they would dig the stuff out of the rocks, quarrying the veins until they were exhausted . . .

But she was only one, and he was taller than her and stronger. He began to hurry after her. She turned and waited at the end of the beach; drawing closer he saw her cupped hands piled with stones.

'Why do you want so many?' he asked, his voice cracking slightly with tension.

She smiled sweetly and said: 'I've collected them for you. It's you that needs so many, isn't it?' She poured them towards him and he caught them all anyhow, scrambling for them and filling his pockets. He didn't thank her. He didn't think she'd done it to be kind.

They climbed a slope at the back of the beach and walked along the top of the cliffs until they came to the little bay where she had left her boat.

'You'll be going now?' he said, making it only half a question.

'Are you coming for that ride?' she countered.

'I don't like boats that are so fast and noisy.'

'How can you know what you like, if you haven't a boat yourself and you've never been off the island?' Her eyes widened searchingly. 'And you said no boats ever come here – how do you know what a boat is at all?'

He felt a deep uneasiness, quickly masked by anger.

'What I know is *my* business!' he said. 'I've shown you the island; I've shown you everything. You've got what you came for. Now go. I live here alone because I like to *be* alone. I don't want visitors. I don't want to see you again!'

She had backed away during his outburst. Now she laughed, a little shakily, and said: 'Right. Goodbye.'

He turned and left the beach. Soon he heard her engine start, shattering the silence. He waited until the roar had faded a little and then judged it safe to look round. She was going full speed for Eldin without a backward glance.

*

Bruce, waking, knew at once that he was not alone; but it took him a minute to locate Deena, sitting on the floor behind his chair.

'What – what are you doing here?' he asked. His voice was sluggish and so was his brain.

Deena didn't reply. Her head was sunk too low for him to see her face properly, but she breathed like someone asleep. Her legs were stretched out and her arms rested limply over them. On the floor near one hand lay two of the striped seeds; proof, if he needed it, of what he had already begun to guess. He bent instinctively and snatched them away; then, growing more sensible, he also moved the rest of the pile from the shelf to his pocket. How right he had been to think he ought to take more care of them!

His movements hadn't woken her; he would have to be more harsh. No use her thinking she could snooze for ever in his shed. He grasped her shoulder and shook it, saying loudly at the same time: 'Come on, Deena, wake up!'

She groaned and opened her eyes, looking at him with alarm or simple astonishment, he wasn't sure which.

'I want to talk to you,' he said.

'Was I asleep?' she asked, recovering fast.

'Yes.'

She began to stand up, looking carefully at the ground as she did so.

'If you're wondering what's happened to the seeds, I've got them,' he said, and noticed with satisfaction her little start of guilt. He also noticed the folded anorak on which she had been sitting – so she'd made herself comfortable first, she hadn't been taken by surprise! 'You knew, didn't you?' he exclaimed. 'You knew they'd send you to sleep!'

'Yes, and you knew *why* I was asleep,' she retorted. 'Why did you wake me? I didn't you, before.'

63

'Before?' Taken aback by her indignation, he was slow to realise what she meant.

'It was one of the best bits of my dream, I was in a speed-boat.'

'*You!*' He could make sense of this all right. 'You – you were the girl who came to the island!'

She said slowly: 'And you were the boy.'

'I couldn't understand why I should dream about you.' His resentment burst out afresh as he thought of it. 'Well, now I know.'

Deena objected: 'She isn't *exactly* me, that girl. Any more than the boy is exactly you – he's better looking, for a start.'

'You would notice something like that,' he said scornfully.

She glared. 'Well, he's certainly just as nasty!'

'The remedy's simple – don't go staring at my seeds and getting into my dreams.'

Deena said: 'But what are they, those seeds? Where did you get them?' Her voice was calmer, as though she had decided to ignore his present nastiness.

It couldn't hurt to tell her. 'They came from that plant. The one you made fun of.'

'Did I?'

'In the middle of the radishes.'

'Oh, that great weed!'

'It may have been a weed, I don't know. It wasn't anything I've ever seen before. It had a big white flower, rather like – oh well, you've seen them, of course – ' He paused, struck by the oddness of the situation. 'Those big white flowers on the island.'

'The ones she picked, and he didn't like it!'

'Of course he wouldn't, they're special.'

'Oh goodness – ' said Deena, 'isn't it odd? How can two people share a dream like that? I wonder what'll happen next time?'

64

'What do you mean, next time?' All Bruce's hostility returned with a rush.

Deena was taken aback. 'Well . . . oh, we are going to try it again, aren't we?'

'*I* probably am,' said Bruce carelessly. '*We* aren't.'

'But that's mean!' she blazed.

'Yes I know, I'm nasty. They're my seeds, though, and if I don't want you, I mean that girl, in my dreams, and I certainly don't – '

She interrupted before his sentence could reach its climax. 'You pig! You rotten slimy selfish little *pig*!'

'Don't be ridiculous,' he said in the iciest voice he could manage. Oddly, it was the least insulting word he minded most; she was nearly a head shorter than him, how dare she call him little?

Deena folded her arms and tried to be dignified. 'All right. We'll see.'

'You needn't think you'll get the chance again,' he warned. 'I'm going to take very good care of the seeds in future.'

Deena looked for the first time at the empty shelf, and he put a protective hand into his pocket, half expecting her to fly at him. When younger they had often come to blows; but she probably realised a fight, like a race, was something he would win easily now. Anyway, she didn't try it. 'I hope they give you nightmares,' she said bitterly; and walked out of the shed.

He didn't want to follow immediately, but when he looked at his watch he saw he had no choice if he was to avoid a scene with his mother. They needn't walk together, though. He hurried past her without speaking, determined to run if necessary; however, she allowed him to stay ahead all the way home.

'You were a long while,' said his mother.

'Well, you know how it is with weeds,' he said, purposely vague.

'I hope you've left enough time for your homework.'

'I'll get it done.'

'Your hands don't look very dirty.'

'There's a tap down there, actually.'

'Hmm.' She sounded suspicious. He wished he'd thought of dirtying his hands.

Voices floated across the street.

'Deena, wherever have you been? Marian came round for you ages ago. Where were you?' Mrs Reevy asked.

Deena's answer was clear and defiant. 'Down at the allotment, helping Bruce!'

'Some help,' sniffed Mrs Payne, 'if it made the job take six times as long. Why didn't you tell me Deena was with you?'

'Last time I said that, you didn't believe me.' Bruce replied sulkily, glad his behaviour was now apparently understandable to his mother, but reluctant to feel any gratitude towards Deena.

'Oh don't be so silly. Last time you said it it wasn't true.'

And I wish it wasn't true this time either, thought Bruce.

6

Bruce put the seeds into an empty cocoa tin, and kept the tin at the back of a drawer. He left them untouched for a couple of days. He couldn't decide what to do about using them again. In one way it seemed obvious that the best place for dreaming would be his own bed; but each evening when he thought of lying there and getting them out he felt nervous. Suppose the dream lasted all night – well, that wouldn't matter, he'd enjoy a long spell on the island, and there'd be no fear of the girl intruding now that he'd settled Deena – but suppose he didn't wake next morning? Of course that wasn't likely; the longest dream he'd had so far had been only two hours, so probably the effect of the seeds would wear off after about that long, and he would just slide into normal sleep. All the same he felt reluctant to try it.

He managed to avoid Deena until Sunday, when he got caught by Mrs Reevy outside church after Mass.

'I hear the allotment's doing fine,' she said.

He wondered uneasily who she'd heard it from – his own mother, or Deena? It wasn't doing anything as far as he knew, unless the lettuces and radishes were through – he'd forgotten to look, last time he'd been there.

'I've promised to get your mother some onion sets,' Mrs Reevy went on. 'I know a place that does them very cheaply. I'll bring them round one day next week, or Deena will. Deena, aren't you going to say hallo?'

67

Deena, who had been standing behind her mother busily ignoring Bruce, narrowed her eyes at him and said: 'Had any good dreams lately?'

Bruce felt himself blush and was furious, partly because she'd mentioned the subject at all and partly because he felt she guessed he hadn't dared to use the seeds since removing them from the shed. He made up his mind to get them out that night.

He went up earlier than usual, telling his mother he was going to read in bed. He thought conditions ought to be as near as possible to what they had been on the other occasions; he didn't want to leave it until he was tired and drowsy.

He took two seeds from the tin. He remembered Deena had found two enough. He put them under his pillow until he was undressed and lying down; then he felt for them, drew them out cupped in one hand, and gazed.

His bed on the island had a single light blanket. Sunlight on his face woke him, and the smell of early morning blowing through the window beside his head. He got up, pulled on his shirt and went down to the sea to bathe.

He thought: *if that girl were here, I wouldn't be able to swim naked like this.* Her intrusion had made him appreciate every detail of his life twice as much. Had it been worth the upset then, he wondered? No, it hadn't. Her second visit in particular had been very disturbing. She had been after something, he was sure; but whatever her purpose he thought he'd succeeded in frustrating it.

The sun wasn't strong enough yet to dry him quickly, and his stomach was empty. He used his shirt as a towel, then knotted it round his waist and walked back through the wood, stopping beside a clump of pale, trailing, tendrilly plants to collect a large handful of dry seedpods.

His favourite goat was waiting by the tower, her two kids playing round the clearing. He fetched a large jug and sat on

68

the doorstep to milk her, talking nonsense to her meanwhile. When the jug was half full he took it inside and the goats wandered away.

He opened his pods and emptied them into a bowl; poured some of the still warm milk on top, and began spooning the mixture into his mouth. The round yellow seeds were hard and brittle, with a sweet, nutty taste. They were very filling.

After his breakfast he went down to get more oil for the lamp; he had noticed it felt rather empty at bedtime the day before. The storeroom was at the bottom of the tower, its door leading off the passage. While he filled the lamp he glanced round at the boxes of candles and clothing, soap and washing powder and tools. It was as well he hadn't let that girl come in here, since she had seemed to think there was something wrong in his possessing all the supplies he would ever need. Also, being so inquisitive, she would have wanted to know why there was another door apparently leading into the spiral staircase, but invisible from the other side. As it was he had kept that secret, and he was glad.

He finished filling the lamp and carried it out of the store-room –

Bruce woke with a jerk, wrenched from one world to another in a most uncomfortable manner. His mother was bending over him, and he thought at first that he must have overslept, as he had feared he might; then he realised it was still night. His bedroom light was on, and his mother – 'Why are you dressed?' he croaked in confusion.

'I haven't gone to bed yet. Are you all right?'

'Of course I am. What time is it?'

'Only ten. I came to see if you'd put your light out.'

'I must have forgotten.'

'Yes, I suppose you must – only you were sleeping so soundly, and you looked rather odd . . .'

'How d'you mean?'

'I don't know exactly.' She was upset and apologetic. 'You look all right now. You do feel all right, don't you?'

'I suppose so,' grumbled Bruce. 'It's not very nice being woken up.'

'I'm sorry. I expect you'll soon get off again, you seem very drowsy. You must have been tired; I didn't really think you'd be asleep yet.'

'Mmm,' said Bruce, exaggerating the drowsiness he genuinely felt so as not to have to talk any more. His mother tucked in the blankets and he yawned and wriggled deeper into the pillow.

'What's this, have you been eating in bed?' she said, removing something from the sheet.

'No, why? Oh, that's mine!' His mother was holding one of the seeds; he almost snatched it from her, alarmed at what might happen if she looked too closely.

'What is it?'

'It's a – well – like a lucky bean, you know. I've got another somewhere.' He groped between the sheets and found it almost at once, to his relief.

'But do you want them in bed with you, nasty hard little things?' His mother was puzzled.

'No – well – p'r'aps not. They can go there.' He put them on his bedside table, pushing them up against a book to keep them from his mother's eyes, and being careful only to give them the merest glance himself.

'You are a funny boy. Said your prayers?'

He made a vague noise. He hadn't, in fact. It was years since she'd asked that particular question. She bent over him again, and for a moment he thought she was going to kiss him; but instead she brushed the hair off his forehead and said: 'Goodnight.'

'Goodnight, Mum.'

She went out, and he gave a great sigh of relief and stretched each of his limbs to its uttermost, undoing all her

70

careful tucking in. He still wasn't sure exactly what had happened, but he felt he'd had a narrow escape in more ways than one. Listening to his mother's footsteps, he waited until they had reached the bottom of the stairs and the sitting room door had closed; then he got up and put the two seeds away in the tin with the others.

He returned to bed, realising he was now wide awake, and lay on his back to think. Obviously he wouldn't be able to risk using the seeds at home again. He wondered in what way he had looked odd while dreaming. He hadn't noticed anything remarkable about Deena when she'd been asleep in the shed; and she hadn't commented on anything strange in his appearance either, though she'd twice had the opportunity of observing him. Maybe his mother's anxiety had just been an example of maternal intuition at work. Of course, he thought suddenly, since his father's death she would be alerted by anything in the way of unnatural sleep. He felt rather guilty that this hadn't occurred to him sooner. Well, it was one more reason for not experimenting again in the house. The shed really was the best place, if it hadn't been for the danger of Deena's prying. At least she wouldn't expect him to use it any more, having seen him remove the seeds.

Two days later Bruce's mother paid an unexpected visit to Mrs Reevy. Visiting between them was normally the other way round; Deena, hearing the effusive welcome with which her mother ushered Mrs Payne into the living room, made a face at Theresa (they were doing the washing up together) and muttered:

'We *are* honoured.'

'Mm?' said Theresa, who hadn't noticed who it was; probably hadn't noticed anyone had arrived at all. No using the back door for Mrs Payne, of course, nothing so familiar.

Mrs Reevy came into the kitchen and put a kettle on,

saying: 'Do me some cups quickly, would you, there isn't a single one clean.'

Deena dried one cup and prodded Theresa into washing another. 'I wonder what she wants,' she said, adding 'Bruce's mother,' to make herself quite clear.

'Something for the garden?' suggested Theresa, not very interested.

'Allotment. Mum *has* got some onion things for her; perhaps she's come to get them.'

She listened. Onions were not being mentioned in the next room, but Bruce was.

'I've been a bit worried about him lately,' said Mrs Payne.

The door wasn't quite closed; Deena put her ear right up to the gap, the teacloth hanging idle in her hand.

'Dee, should you?' objected Theresa.

'Sssh!'

'. . . he just went off to the cemetery. He hadn't said anything to me about it. I was quite worried by the time he got home.'

'Well,' said Mrs Reevy, 'it's not *so* surprising, is it. I know he didn't show much at the time, but it's bound to have affected him, losing his father that way.'

'Yes – that does worry me rather, how much it might have affected him. He gave me such a fright the other night, not that he meant to . . .'

The kettle was beginning to boil. Deena tiptoed across the kitchen and turned down the gas, then darted back to her station by the door. Theresa was listening too now, sliding the dishmop automatically round and round a single plate.

'. . . and as soon as I'd woken him I felt I'd been silly, because he was perfectly all right, but it *wasn't* like him to be asleep so early, and it did look such a heavy sleep . . .'

'But it was nothing, of course!' Mrs Reevy's voice was loud and bracing. 'Oh, I'm sure you don't need to worry in *that* way. Good gracious no. They do get awfully tired at his age, I remember so well the trouble we had with Patricia . . .'

'*And the doctor said she was outgrowing her strength,*' chanted Deena in an undertone, having heard the story many times before. She left the door and resumed drying up, judging that she had had the interesting part of the conversation.

So Bruce had run into trouble using the seeds at home! Serve him right, she thought, dropping cutlery briskly into the drawer. He should have stuck to the shed.

Her mother bustled into the kitchen. 'Isn't that kettle boiling yet? Who turned it down?'

'Oh yes, do you want us to make the tea?' said Deena helpfully.

'I'll do it now. Mind, let me get to the sink.' She moved Theresa aside and emptied out the water she'd used to warm the pot. 'Did you do some cups?'

'Over there. Wake up, dreamy,' said Deena to her sister. 'You've been ten minutes on that plate and I've got nothing to dry.'

Theresa handed her the plate, frowning abstractedly, and Deena shook off the worst of the wet.

'You're splashing my feet,' complained Theresa mildly.

'You should hurry up a bit, then the things would have a chance to drain before I get to them.' She held the door while her mother carried the tray into the next room and shut it when she heard Mrs Payne say politely: 'How *is* Patricia?'

As soon as the door closed Theresa looked at her and asked with unusual directness: 'What was that about Bruce?'

'Couldn't you hear?'

'Yes, I did hear . . . *You* were very interested, weren't you?'

'What if I was?'

'Well, why were you?'

'I wanted to know what had brought her ladyship over here. Why are you so interested, come to that?'

Theresa said slowly: 'It just sounded rather funny to me. If Bruce was sleeping oddly . . . his mother didn't ask him if he'd taken anything, did she?'

'Well, she could see he hadn't as soon as he woke. Anyway, why would he?' scoffed Deena. 'He's not depressed.'

'I don't mean like his father. But you were talking about him the other day, weren't you, and about drugs that make people dream.'

'I didn't talk about it – ' Deena broke off, and arranged her words with care. 'I didn't mention it in connection with Bruce. His name came up because of gardening, and then I thought of dreams because I'd had a good one the night before. Oh come on, *do* wash the rest of the stuff, or I'll go away and you can dry it yourself!'

Theresa's hands began moving again. 'That's not how I remember it,' she said dubiously, but Deena was holding out her hand for the next plate and didn't reply.

'There now,' said Mrs Reevy next day, 'after all that I forgot to give Mrs Payne those onion sets.'

Theresa looked up from her books and said: 'I'll take them across.'

'Will you?' Her mother was surprised. 'Aren't you working?'

'It'll only take a minute. Where are they?' She pushed back her chair, and seeing that she obviously meant it her mother fetched the box from the kitchen.

'There. They ought to go in as soon as possible, if Bruce can manage it.'

Bruce was surprised too when he answered the door and found Theresa on the step.

'These are for your mother,' she said quickly.

'Oh yes. Thanks. She'll be pleased.'

'Isn't she here?'

'She's gone to the shop. I'd have gone, but I'm supposed to be doing my homework.'

'I was doing mine,' said Theresa, a smile glimmering in her eyes.

'You need a break sometimes, don't you?' said Bruce in delighted fellow feeling. 'People do, I mean. Even you.'

'Even me,' agreed Theresa, her smile more pronounced.

'Oh, I didn't mean it to sound like that – by the way, do you want to come in? – I always forget to ask people, Mum gets cross when I keep them standing.'

Theresa did come in, rather flummoxing Bruce, who had expected her to say no, she must go. He closed the door and asked uncertainly:

'Would you like some coffee?'

'Well . . . yes, all right, just quickly, if you're having some.'

He put the kettle on and made a great business of setting out the mugs and finding the milk. He liked Theresa, but she did make him feel rather shy, partly because of the difference in their ages and partly because she was so quiet. Deena would never have let a silence like this develop.

'Oh – those onion things ought to be got in as soon as possible,' said Theresa abruptly. 'So Mum says, anyway.'

'Another job for me,' said Bruce.

'Do you mind?'

She seemed sympathetic, and he said at once: 'Not really. The allotment's quite fun, in a way.'

'Deena seems to think so.'

'Deena?' What on earth had she told them? To his annoyance Bruce felt himself beginning to go red.

'She spent ages helping you down there the other day, didn't she? Her friend what'shername was rather cross.'

'Marian,' said Bruce, relaxing a little at the casualness of Theresa's tone.

'Yes. Do you know her?'

75

'Not really. She wasn't at St Joseph's with us.'

'You were very friendly then, weren't you.'

'Your mother thinks we still are,' said Bruce rather bitterly. 'So does mine.'

'Well,' said Theresa after a pause, 'I know Dee can be a bit much. Maybe you haven't such a lot in common now . . . but I suppose you still stick up for each other – wouldn't tell each other's secrets?'

'We haven't any secrets,' said Bruce, much too fast.

Theresa seemed to notice nothing odd. 'Deena's always been the adventurous one of the family,' she said as though thinking aloud. 'She gets impatient with quieter people, like me.'

'And me.'

Theresa looked at him alertly. 'Yes. It must be difficult sometimes for her friends, when she has one of her wild ideas. I'm afraid she might persuade them to do things they'd rather not.'

'Here's your coffee,' said Bruce. He felt a bit bewildered; she obviously had something on her mind, but what exactly?

'For instance,' said Theresa, not looking at him now, 'the other day she was asking me about dreams, and drugs; opium, and so on . . .'

Bruce nearly laughed.

'Deena hasn't been persuading me to take drugs, if that's what you think.'

'Oh!' Theresa blushed, and he wished he'd put it better; he didn't like to see her at a loss. However, before he could say any more his mother came back from the shop; a good thing really, as the conversation had got itself into such a muddle. Theresa explained about the onions, drank her coffee quickly, and left.

'I hope you remembered to tell Mrs Payne they ought to go in as soon as possible,' said her mother.

'Yes – well, I told Bruce. She wasn't there at first.'

'What took you so long then? I thought you must be chatting.'

'Told Bruce what?' demanded Deena, coming into the room.

'I was talking to Bruce,' said Theresa to her mother. 'We had some coffee.'

'You and Bruce?' said Deena, loud with astonishment. 'Whose idea was that?'

'His, of course.'

'What on earth did you talk about? He's never been *your* friend.'

'Don't be silly, Deena,' said her mother. 'It was very nice of Bruce to offer some coffee – I've always thought he had good manners. I'm sure they found plenty to talk about.'

'I have known him just as long as you, after all,' said Theresa to Deena; and to her mother, agreeing: 'Yes, he is a nice boy.'

Deena made a rude noise and bounced out. It irritated her to hear Theresa and her mother praising Bruce; but it irritated her far more to think that Theresa had been having cosy cups of coffee with him. *She* should have been the one to take the onions across; she would have, if she'd known they were to go; what did Theresa mean by grabbing the job for herself? Though of course Bruce might not have offered *her* any coffee. He hadn't the other night, after they'd pacified Stephen, even though she'd saved his kettle from boiling dry. Come to think of it he'd asked for Theresa first on that occasion, hadn't he? Deena felt herself growing quite angry. Oh, she would have to have a word with him, that was obvious. Theresa might be nearly sixteen, but that didn't mean she was interested in boys, *oh* no. Much too wrapped up in her work.

When she went to bed Deena lay awake in the room they shared until Theresa came up (not difficult, as Theresa was never late) and then asked at once: 'What *did* you and Bruce talk about?'

'Mm?' said Theresa.

'Oh, you heard,' said Deena impatiently. 'You and Bruce, with your coffee; what did you talk about?'

Theresa yawned and said: 'You, mostly.'

'*Me?*' said Deena, floundering between outrage and satisfaction.

'Well, I was worried,' said Theresa defensively, 'and I thought you were a bit funny when Mrs Payne came last night.'

'You went on at him about drugs!' cried Deena.

'Ssh,' said Theresa, embarrassed.

'You did, didn't you?'

'I did just touch on the subject.'

'And what did he say?'

'Oh, what I ought to have known – that he wouldn't dream of trying anything, even if you wanted him to.'

'If *I* wanted him to!'

'Do hush, Dee, you'll wake the younger ones.'

'Well, what a nerve,' fumed Deena, nearly adding, *You've got it the wrong way round entirely.* But that would only start Theresa on her questions again, just when Bruce had successfully put her off. And made her feel a bit silly too, Deena guessed. Serve her right. And serve Bruce right, the awkward minutes he must have suffered, for asking her to coffee in the first place.

7

'And you don't think it'll take you too long to plant them?' said Mrs Payne the following evening.

'No,' said Bruce. 'I haven't got much homework today anyway.' And they had to be planted, and he didn't want his mother suggesting she did it herself. Somehow he didn't fancy the idea of her going down to the allotment. It was his place.

He set off carrying the box carefully in front of him, like a tray. In his pocket was his tin of seeds. He had taken them from the drawer on an impulse just after changing his shoes. He hadn't really been intending to use them today, but if he didn't run into Deena anywhere on the way to the allotment, then maybe . . .

He didn't see her in the street, and she wasn't at the swings; today they were occupied entirely by younger children. Stephen Waddilove was there; he came up to Bruce and said: 'Where are you going?'

'To do some gardening,' said Bruce, a little surprised to be asked.

'Can I come?'

Bruce was on the point of agreeing when he remembered the tin in his pocket. 'Not this time, I don't think,' he said.

'When can I?'

'Well — I don't know. We'll see. It isn't any fun, you know. It's boring.'

'This place is boring,' said Stephen gloomily. 'They won't let me go on the roundabout.'

'Well – ' said Bruce again. He looked at the roundabout, identified Linda Reevy among the spinning passengers, and called: 'Hey, Linda, you might let Stephen on.'

'No room!' said Linda, and all the other children took up the chant. 'No room! No room!'

With the roundabout in motion it was hard to tell whether or not this was true. Bruce gave up, saying: 'You could go on the horse.' The horse was in the charge of a young woman who was giving two toddlers a gentle ride; she'd be sure to let Stephen on, but it wouldn't be much fun. Stephen turned away rather dispiritedly, not speaking, and Bruce didn't wait to see whether he followed his suggestion or not.

When Deena came past half an hour later, Stephen was sitting on one of the swings, moving himself slightly by kicking at the ground. Angela, the same age, had been able to propel herself on a swing for some time; but Stephen had not mastered the art, and he had nobody to push him.

Deena was carrying a watering can. Stephen noticed it and ran up to her, saying eagerly: 'Are you going to do gardening? Bruce is doing gardening. He told me.'

'I know,' said Deena. 'I'm going to help.'

From her bedroom window she had caught sight of Bruce a little earlier, carrying a box down the road, and had guessed his destination. She and Marian had at the time been creating new hairstyles for each other, but soon afterwards Deena had lost interest in this occupation to such an extent that Marian had gone home earlier than intended. It had occurred to Deena then that if Bruce was doing some planting he would need the watering can. Also, she wanted a private word with him about the night when he'd used the seeds at home. If Theresa could talk to him about it, not knowing half the facts, he couldn't possibly refuse to discuss it with Deena; or so she reasoned.

'I'd like to help too,' said Stephen now, in a hopeful voice.

'Oh no,' said Deena quickly. 'I don't think you could.'

'I'd like to do gardening. I wouldn't be bored.'

'*We* would though, if we had you along.'

Stephen bent his head and kicked at a tuft of grass. Deena, feeling slightly ashamed of her sharpness, put one hand on his hair for a moment and then took it away; it felt unattractively rough, like the pelt of a not very clean animal. 'Go and play,' she said more kindly. 'Or ask your mother to let you do some digging at home. You haven't got the sort of garden you could spoil.'

Stephen still didn't answer or look at her. She decided she had spent enough time on him and hurried on.

The allotment was apparently deserted, but when she got closer she could see the onions had been planted; and Bruce couldn't have gone home or Stephen would have noticed him passing the swings. He must be in the shed. Which probably meant she wouldn't be able to talk to him after all.

She could look, anyway. She went confidently towards the shed, a helpful girl with a watering can as far as any watcher was concerned. A gentle knock received no reply, and she opened the door. He was there, just as she'd expected; nevertheless her heart gave a small jump at the sight of him sprawled in the chair with his eyes closed.

She went inside and closed the door behind her. Her heart was still jumping, and she couldn't pretend she didn't know why. Somewhere about him would be the seeds; this was her chance to get into the dream world again. Lost in sleep as he was, he couldn't possibly stop her.

The seeds weren't on the shelf. In his hand then, or fallen from his fingers. Not on the floor. His right hand lay palm up, empty; his left was loosely curled at his side. She bent closer and saw the glint of colour between his leg and the chair arm. Very delicately she picked up the seed. Would one be enough? Try it and see.

On her third visit to the island the girl approached more carefully than before. When she judged she was near enough she switched off her engine and allowed a convenient current to carry her towards the shore. She used a paddle for the last few yards, anchored the boat in the small bay and waded ashore. She had seen no sign of the boy, and she hoped he had not seen her. Now that she was here she was in no hurry to meet him.

The goats weren't so interested in her without him; they were unafraid, but not particularly friendly. She saw the path that led to the tower and turned in the other direction, towards the wilder end of the island – a jumble of rocks, bushes, and small trees. She was hungry, she found. She felt in her pocket, making sure she had her knife.

It was some time later when the boy found the boat. He stood and stared at it, first incredulous and then angry. She had paid no attention to his words – she was here again! But where? Nowhere very close, he quickly realised. The beach, and the grass behind it, obviously didn't contain her. And if she had looked for him in the tower she would have found him, or at least met him on his way here. Perhaps she wanted to avoid him.

Why had she come? What was she up to? He must find her; he would have no peace until he did. If she had come for pieces of the coloured stone she would be at the beach with the special rocks. On the other hand if she simply wanted to hide, she would probably be at the scrubby end of the island. He paused, undecided which direction to try first. Suppose he chose wrongly, and in the meantime she returned to the boat and escaped without any confrontation? That wouldn't do.

The boat must be dealt with, and he thought he saw how. His plan depended on being able to move it without using the engine; wading out to it, he found it had its own paddle. So far so good.

A candle and matches were necessary; he hurried back to the tower to fetch them. There was still no sign of the girl when he returned. As he pulled up the anchor he hoped she wouldn't catch him in the act of paddling away; it was no more than she deserved, but he would find his behaviour awkward to explain.

Nothing happened, however. There were no cries from the shore. He took the boat out of the bay and along the foot of the cliffs until he reached the half submerged entrance to a cave. It was invisible from above because of the overhang. He moored the boat about twenty yards inside, by a rocky ledge. The dim watery light was just sufficient here for him to be able to see what he was doing.

He lit a candle for the next stage of his journey, and set out along a narrow rocky passage which started from the back of the ledge, and ended half a mile away in a flight of steps. The steps spiralled upwards; they were the underground portion of his tower staircase, and were divided from it by a wall at ground level. He emerged through a door into his storeroom, feeling very satisfied with the last hour's work. He had always felt the cave might be useful one day.

Now that the boat was secure there was less need to hurry. He ate and drank before setting out on his search for the girl; he also supplied himself with a stick. It wasn't exactly a weapon, but he felt it gave him a certain appearance of authority.

He went first to the beach with the coloured stones. It was deserted, and he moved on to the wild end of the island. He hadn't gone far over the rougher ground when he paused to sniff. He could smell wood smoke.

He hurried forward, angry and afraid. A fire on the island could do immense damage if it got out of control. Now he could see the smoke ahead, a single rising spiral; and topping a small rise, he also saw the girl.

She had in fact sited her fire very sensibly, in a hollow among some rocks; but his relief at this lasted only as long as it took him to realise why she had needed a fire in the first place. She had used it to cook; and what she had cooked she must first have killed. There were small bones lying beside the embers.

She had her back to him, but at his involuntary exclamation she turned her head.

'Oh,' she said. 'It's you.'

'What have you done?' he demanded.

'I wanted another look at the island. Do you mind?'

He struggled for words.

'I mind *that*,' he said, pointing at the bones.

'Rabbit,' she said. 'I was hungry. Would you like some? I didn't eat it all – it would make a change from your usual fruit and nuts. You'd find them very easy to catch, if you wanted to add them to your diet.'

He was nearly choked with rage. 'Of course they're easy to catch,' he got out. 'They're tame. All the creatures on the island are. I never touch them. There's plenty here to eat without that. You could have found other food if you'd tried.'

The girl was standing now. She seemed to have realised his mood.

'I didn't know you felt so strongly about it,' she said. 'Anyway, it was only one.'

He looked at her, unspeaking, until she dropped her eyes to the fire.

'That'll go out soon,' she said, half to herself. 'It doesn't need smothering. Well – I'd better leave, maybe.'

She began to walk slowly away. He called after her: 'Why did you come?'

'Oh . . . because I wanted to,' she replied.

84

Looking again at the pathetic pile of bones, he recalled the fact which his outrage had put out of his head. He shouted: 'You won't find your boat where you left it!'

She stopped dead, and said sharply: 'What do you mean?'

'Go and see.'

She began to run. He was glad to be left alone. He would fetch her boat for her, but in his own time. There were other things to do first.

He had nothing with him which he could have used to dig a hole; he placed the rabbit's bones in the middle of the smouldering ashes and covered everything with rocks. There were plenty there. The flat layer looked unfinished, so he began to build it into a cairn. He worked slowly and carefully, the effort soothing his anger. When it was finished he stood and eyed it with a certain sad pleasure, meanwhile flexing his aching muscles. It would stand here for ever, a monument to the only creature on the island harmed by a human being. He didn't realise how long the task had taken until the girl reappeared. She was hot and dishevelled, and her voice was desperate.

'Where is it? I've been all round the island. What have you done with it?'

He said: 'I've buried it.'

She looked from him to the cairn and said flatly: 'You're mad.'

He didn't reply.

'I'm talking about my *boat*,' she said, her voice beginning to rise again. 'What have you done with it? Have you hurt it?'

'Boats don't have feelings.'

'Neither do bloody rabbits.'

He made himself wait before asking: 'I suppose it enjoyed being killed?'

'*What have you done with my boat?*'

He didn't want to tell her, he discovered. He quite liked

85

seeing her distress. 'Oh, I got rid of it,' he said casually.

'What do you mean?'

'You got rid of my rabbit. I got rid of your boat.'

She stared for a moment; then turned and went away at a wild plunging run. He watched, expecting her to lose her footing amid the rocks, but she was still upright when she vanished.

He was suddenly very tired. He sat down on the ground.

. . and woke to find himself in the old chair. Deena was the one on the floor. She had to be here, of course; how else would the girl have got back to the island? He thought: 'Why can't she *leave me alone*?'

It was because of the seeds, he realised. Perhaps he should give her one or two and let her go away and dream her dreams by herself. But he knew he would never do that. He wasn't sure why.

She was still asleep; running round the island, searching for signs of her boat? He put out a hand, then drew it back. Facing each other wouldn't be easy after a dream like that. Better, perhaps, to avoid a meeting. She had complained before because he woke her; well, this time he would leave her alone.

He closed the door of the shed very gently behind him and set off for home. Halfway up the path he looked back; the shed was still closed.

His street was full of playing children, and as he drew near to his own house Stephen Waddilove planted himself right in his path and said: 'I looked for you.'

'Looked for me?' asked Bruce warily. 'Why?'

'I did. I looked for you where the gardens are but you weren't there. Deena wasn't either.'

'Mum wants Deena,' said Linda Reevy. 'Deena was supposed to do the washing up. There's going to be a row when she gets home.'

She was staring at him in a nasty inquisitive way, waiting for a reaction.

'Deena's always in a row, isn't she?' he replied in a rather hearty voice.

'You weren't there,' said Stephen singlemindedly. 'Where were you?'

'Go away,' muttered Bruce. Edging round him, he tried to reach his own gate; but as he did so he was hailed by Mrs Reevy.

'Oh, Bruce! Is Deena with you?'

'No – no, I haven't seen her,' he replied, much too quickly; thinking only that nobody must go looking for her in the shed.

'Didn't she catch you, then?' she said, puzzled. 'She was coming to help, down at the allotment.'

'She told me,' said Stephen, his voice a slow gloomy bass under the shriller agitation of the other speakers. 'I saw her go by. First I saw Bruce and then I saw Deena. But when I went back to look for them . . .'

'She did come of course, yes!' said Bruce, drowning him. 'Quite a while ago, that was.' (Was it? Yes, it must have been.) 'I don't know where she is now.'

'Well, I hope she turns up soon.' Mrs Reevy sounded vexed.

'Yes,' said Bruce politely, and hurried indoors to deal with the usual remarks from his mother about the length of time he had been away.

After she had left the boy beside his ridiculous cairn, the girl ran all the way to the beach where she had anchored her boat and searched, hopelessly, for any sign of what he might have done to it. There was no wreckage; nothing. Probably he had simply set it adrift, in which case there was no use looking for it now. All the same she stared out to sea for some time, her eyes burning.

When she left the beach she took the path to the tower. The boy might be there by now. She entered without knocking and crashed up the spiral staircase, glancing into every room and shouting to him as she went. Even when it was obvious he wasn't there she continued her climb, only slowing a little for lack of breath.

Near the top she found a room that stopped her. It was very light and bare, and every surface held objects carved from translucent coloured stone. So he had made all these! She moved among them, lifting one here and there to feel the balance and finger the delicate workmanship. Her mood had quietened without her realising it, until she came suddenly on the carved boat which he had shown to her before. She snatched it up, the fury of her loss possessing her with new force; and before she quite knew what she was doing she had hurled it across the room. It hit the far wall and broke into three pieces. She sent a bowl after it and then something else – she didn't look, just grabbed the nearest things to hand, moving round the room in a whirl of destruction until the floor was littered with coloured fragments that crunched beneath her feet.

As abruptly as she had begun, she stopped. She looked at what she had done and was appalled. Her breath was coming in gasps, but when she left the room she descended the stairs at top speed, falling over her feet in her anxiety to be gone. If the boy returned before she got to the bottom she would be well and truly caught.

She collapsed as soon as she reached the sheltering trees, crouching on the ground and panting with relief at her escape. If indeed it could be called an escape.

For the first time she saw her situation clearly. She no longer had a boat; she was trapped on the island. With the boy.

She jumped violently at an unexpected noise, then realised it was only a bleat. Some of the goats were in the clearing.

Maybe they came there to be milked. The boy would be back soon in any case; he would discover what she had done.

She must hide, but where? What was she to do?

Deena woke, and at once felt a twofold relief; first because the dream (or nightmare?) was over, and second because she was alone. Then she thought that the latter circumstance was rather odd. Where was Bruce? He must have seen her when he woke. Why slip away? Hadn't he wanted to talk? Well, in view of the dream perhaps that wasn't surprising. They must talk some time though; they couldn't just behave as if nothing had happened.

She stood up, and catching sight of the seed she had borrowed lying on the floor, pounced on it with satisfaction. He must have left in a great hurry if he'd forgotten to remove that. He would be upset when he realised. He would want to see her, to ask her for it back. Well, he could ask; but he wouldn't get it. Even if she never used it again (and with the memory of the last dream fresh in her mind she couldn't believe she would) she had it now and she intended to keep it.

A glance at her watch sent her speeding home. How to explain her absence? Still, one good thing; by now the washing up had probably been done by somebody else.

It had, and her mother (the person in question) was not at all pleased with her.

'I'm sorry,' said Deena, 'but it took so long, helping Bruce.'

'That's not what he said.'

'Oh!' Deena was taken aback. 'What did he say, then?'

'That you were only there for a short while, and he hadn't seen you since.'

'*Did* he,' said Deena, her temper rising. 'Well, we were together all the while; he left me there when he went, and he jolly well knows he did.'

Her mother look doubtful. 'But I asked him where you were. Why should he tell a fib?'

'Because he's not so jolly perfect as you think!'

'Deena,' said her mother automatically; then: 'But *why* did he leave you there?'

'I was finishing things off.'

'Well, it all sounds very odd to me. Had you quarrelled or something?'

'You could say that, I suppose.'

'Well, had you or hadn't you?'

'Yes!' shouted Deena. 'We'd quarrelled! Now are you satisfied?' Slamming out of the room, she ran upstairs and lay on her bed, where (most uncharacteristically, for her) she shed a few tears into the pillow.

8

It was not until he was undressing on the same day that Bruce realised some of the seeds might be missing. He found the tin in his pocket; he had forgotten to put it back in the drawer when he got home, distracted first by Mrs Reevy's enquiries about Deena and then by his own mother wanting to know why he'd left so little time for the doing of his homework. In the end the only way to satisfy her had been to say that he had taken a long time because he'd been working out in his head the plan of an essay they'd been set. On blood sports, he'd said, and had felt this added rather a neat touch to his fabrication; though afterwards he was sorry he'd made a joke, however private, about the death of the rabbit.

As he put the tin back into the drawer he wondered rather hopelessly what place he could find for dreaming now. Home was no good, the shed was no good; he'd thought he'd been careful enough getting there, but Deena must have known or guessed where he was or she wouldn't have followed him. And how had she managed to get hold of any seeds to use herself? She must have removed them from his sleeping hand – and at this point he realised, with a horrible sinking of his heart, that he had not done the same to her. He had gone away and let her keep them.

He had never counted the seeds, so there was no point in counting them now. What he did remember was that he had only taken three or four out of the tin to use; and before leaving the shed he had picked up three seeds from the seat of the chair, so it seemed Deena almost certainly hadn't got more than one. But that was small comfort. One was obviously all she needed.

He must make her give it back. How, though? He had never been able to make Deena do anything, and if he let her see that he wanted it she would probably insist on keeping it just to be perverse. He would need to be crafty.

The plan which came into his head then was, he thought modestly, rather a gem of craftiness. It would use against Deena her own infuriating behaviour. He wished he could put it into action at once; but he had to wait until the following evening.

'I'm just going to do a bit of weeding down at the allotment,' he told his mother after tea; and to forestall her objections added: 'I'll take my French book with me; we've got to revise for a test, and I can do it down there.'

'While you're weeding?' said his mother blankly. 'How can you possibly?'

'No, I mean afterwards – I might work for a bit in the shed.'

'But the shed's no place for that kind of work, Bruce, don't be silly. You need to be at a table in a proper light.'

'I don't need a table for *reading* – and there's bags of light; I can sit by the window.'

'In the old chair, I suppose.' His mother pursed her lips. 'I don't think the fact that your father used to do that is any reason for you to do the same.'

'That's not my reason. Anyway,' (Bruce allowed himself to be diverted) 'you don't know what he used to do. He might have just sat there to think, or – or to draw, or anything.'

One of Mr Payne's spasmodic interests had been sketching. Somewhere in the house there must still be books full of his small intricate drawings, but Bruce hadn't seen them since his father died.

'And I thought I told you the chair was to come back here?' his mother said.

'It would be terribly awkward carrying it all that way – it would take ages.'

'Your father managed it apparently.'

'Well, I think I'd need someone to help me. I'll do it one day in the holidays, I'll get a friend to help.'

He left the house quickly, not giving his mother time to consider the unlikelihood of this event. He never asked any of his school friends home; he couldn't really picture himself doing so for the first time simply in order to gain their assistance with the shifting of such a dilapidated piece of furniture.

Looking across at the Reevys' house he wondered if Deena was inside. It would be infuriating if on the one occasion when he wanted her to know where he was she somehow didn't find it out. Stephen Waddilove was playing on the pavement and Bruce considered telling him, very loudly, that he was just off to do a bit of weeding – but then Stephen might start pestering to come with him. So he said nothing, even avoiding Stephen's eye as he walked past.

It would have been to no purpose anyway, he found, because Deena was at the swings with Marian and another girl. Should he say hello or not? Which would be more like his usual self – no, which would be more likely to have the effect he wanted?

The girls settled his conflict by calling a cheeky greeting, to which he replied in an offhand growl. Then on to the allotment, not glancing back; into the shed and into the chair.

Now. Move the tin to the back pocket of his trousers – a bit uncomfortable, but it had to be somewhere Deena couldn't get at it. Although she had one seed already you could never rely on moderation in Deena. Lean back, fold his arms, close his eyes. Would she come? Surely. She would stick to her usual interfering habits, and they would result in her downfall. He concentrated on breathing slowly and deeply.

It seemed a very long while until he heard her at the door, and when he did a sudden misgiving nearly jerked him out of his careful pose – suppose she wasn't alone? It required an immense amount of self-control not to peep.

She came in very quietly. No whispering. She must be alone. The floorboards creaked as she moved around; creaked in a new way which suggested she had sat down. Wanting to hold his breath, he remembered just in time that he mustn't, in case she noticed.

Stillness followed, but he waited a few more minutes before he risked opening his eyes. It was all right; she was sound asleep. And the missing seed lay in her lap. He made a quick grab and repossessed himself of it, feeling a great wave of satisfaction and he put it into the tin with the others.

She slept on, undisturbed. It was odd to look at her and think that in a way she wasn't here at all; or at least (he amended) Deena was here, but her other self was – where? In her boat? No, she couldn't be; she must still be on the island, she had no means of getting off. Suddenly he didn't like the idea of her being there when he wasn't. He leaned towards her.

'Wake up,' he said; then, louder: 'Deena! Wake up!'

Nothing happened. He put one hand on her arm, but she didn't stir. Finally he knelt beside her and shook her – only for a few moments, because there was something alarming in the way her head rolled about on her shoulders, and in her general lack of response. He was quite relieved to note, when he let go, that she was definitely breathing. She had felt almost like a corpse.

He sat back on his heels and considered. Could it be that the effect of the seeds was stronger at first – that a person who had recently looked at them was impossible to wake

94

until it had had time to begin wearing off? If so he had been extremely lucky when he had used them at home. What on earth would his mother have done if she'd tried to rouse him while he was in the same state as Deena now? The thought sent cold stabs through his middle.

He looked at her again. If she couldn't be woken, he might as well go away and leave her; but he didn't want to. He still didn't altogether like the idea of her being on the island without him.

He glanced at the tin of seeds, and realised that there was another possibility. If she couldn't be got off the island, he had better go there himself.

The boy was surprised to hear the goats bleating beside the tower as he came home. It must be even later than he'd thought; the business of the girl and the rabbit had used up a whole afternoon.

He greeted his favourite goat and went inside to fetch a jug. Something bothered him vaguely on the stairs, but he didn't realise what until he had finished milking and was taking the jug up to his living room. It was the doors – every door was open, even those to rooms he never used. Could that girl have been here while he was away?

He dumped the jug and went on up, looking now into each room as he came to it. He didn't know what he expected to find – certainly nothing as dreadful as the scene of destruction which finally met his eyes.

He was dazed. He could do nothing but stare. He had the vague impression that some pieces were undamaged, but he couldn't bring himself to go and search among the fragments to find out which. He might later; at the moment a closer inspection would be unbearable.

Eventually he managed to move, closing the door on the unspeakable mess and continuing slowly upwards. The rest of the tower held no surprises; nor, when he looked from the top of it, could he see any sign of the girl anywhere on the island.

The sun had set. It would soon be dark. Whatever he did about the girl must wait until the morning; there was only one action that could be taken immediately, and this he did as soon as it occurred to him – he went down to the store-room, took a bunch of keys which were hanging on a nail, and closed and locked the outer door of the tower.

He couldn't eat; he didn't want to think. He drank a little milk and went to bed.

The girl spent the night near the spring. She was very thirsty, and finding it seemed almost more important than avoiding the boy; but once she had reached it (by a mixture of memory and luck) she decided it was a good place to be for other reasons. Because she was on high ground she would have warning of the boy's approach from any direction; and there was a sheltered corner where she could sit with her back to a rock. And of course water was no problem as long as she remained here.

She meant to stay awake, but sleep overcame her in the end. She woke in the dawn – cold, stiff, and hungry. A drink of water did very little to satisfy her stomach. She remembered the boy had said there was plenty of food growing here, and went to see what she could find.

It wasn't easy. There were fruits and berries, but none that she recognised. How was she to know which were safe to eat? She gathered a handful of striped seeds from what she thought had been, when in flower, the large white daisies which the boy hadn't wanted her to pick; but she did it mostly as an act of defiance. She didn't dare assume they were edible. The only food she could definitely recollect be-ing given by him was a kind of yellow root, and she hadn't time to pull up every plant she came to in search of it. And when she thought what had happened since killing the rabbit, to her boat and to the boy's carvings, there seemed very little point in trying to abide by his taboos. Another rabbit was the obvious breakfast.

She had to go to the wild end of the island to find any. She skirted the tower as widely as possible, glad of the knife in her hand. When she reached the rough grass and rocks the rabbits were there, browsing in the dew; still as tame as the day before, though she wondered how long that would last. She selected her target and approached on soft feet.

She was nearly there when a sharp blow in the small of her back made her fall to the ground. Dizzy with pain and shock she looked up and saw the boy approaching with a stone in one hand. He had obviously just thrown a similar missile. Immediately she grabbed for her knife, but it had landed some way away, and when she tried to reach it she was prevented by a new pain in her ankle; the boy got to it first, and picked it up.

'Are you hurt?' he asked, not coming any closer.

She gritted her teeth. 'What do you think?'

'I think you were going to kill another rabbit.'

She didn't reply.

'Can you stand?'

'I expect so.' She wasn't going to try with him watching.

'I'd better help you back to the tower.'

'*No*.' Her ankle was sprained, not broken. She would be able to crawl. 'Just go away and leave me alone.'

'I can't do that,' he said reasonably. 'I'm sorry I hurt you; but you had to be stopped.' He glanced at the knife he held, weighed it for a moment in his hand, and then hurled it away.

'That's a good knife!'

'It can be collected later,' he said. 'I'm not coming near you with it, that's all. You might try to grab it while I'm helping you along.'

She would have; he was right. She made a sudden violent attempt to stand, wanting to do it without his assistance and managing it. She couldn't get her balance though, and would have fallen straight away if he hadn't been there to support her.

The walk to the tower was grim. The boy's helpfulness was harder to endure than his aggression. Neither spoke; she didn't even know whether he had discovered yet what she had done to his treasures.

He settled this question when they arrived. Having hoisted her up several turns of the staircase and into a room that was almost totally bare, he took her across to the only piece of furniture (a bed) and said as she sat thankfully on the edge of it:

'There's nothing in here you can damage.'

Her reply was to massage first her ankle and then her back; while doing this she needn't meet his eye, and it would perhaps remind him that he had taken steps to even the score.

'I'll bring you some food,' he said.

'I don't feel hungry any more.'

'You will, though,' he said calmly. He went out, closing the heavy door behind him, and she heard the rattle of a bunch of keys. The sound jerked her to her feet, exhausted as she was; she limped across the room and tried the latch. It was as she dreaded. She was locked in.

Deena woke, and found that Bruce was waking too. As usual he was taking longer to surface; she had stood up and was shaking out her anorak when his eyes focussed on her in recognition.

It was no use, she thought, trying to pretend that the dream hadn't happened. Actually the fate of the boy's carvings had been on her mind ever since the previous dream. The girl hadn't apologised, but Deena could.

'I'm sorry,' she said.

She was immediately sorrier still that she'd spoken; because Bruce's response was a smirk. Small, but a definite smirk.

'Oh, that's all right,' he said. 'I've got it back.'

'Got what back?'

'The seed, of course.'

'That!' She couldn't help glancing at the floor, which was bare. Then she remembered they had woken together, and looked more closely at the area where she'd been sitting in case it was a bluff. 'How could you have? When?' she asked.

'Almost as soon as you came in. I wasn't asleep, you know. I was waiting for you.'

His triumph was disgusting.

'Well, you jolly well slept afterwards,' she spat, 'and I hope you liked what you found!' Forget the apology. Bury it. The boy deserved all he got, and so did Bruce.

Her words were sinking in. He turned red, but didn't answer.

'And if you think I want your rotten seeds you're mistaken!' she continued. 'I can do very well without being locked up in your tower, thank you very much!'

'Thank *you*,' he said, 'if you mean you're really going to keep away in future.'

'I won't come within *miles*,' she said, and left the shed.

She had certainly meant the words when she said them; but even as she stormed up the path to the swings she was beginning to wonder. The question that exercised her brain was what would happen to the girl in the tower if Bruce was allowed to dream a dream by himself? How could she be there, if Deena wasn't dreaming? On the other hand how could she not be, since she was locked in?

Probably she would be there, but invisible. For the duration of the dream the boy would ignore his prisoner. And that would suit Bruce very well, thought Deena angrily; he wouldn't care if the girl stagnated in that tower for ever, just so long as she didn't bother him.

Pat and Marian weren't still at the swings, thank goodness. When she'd left them she had pretended to remember a message from her mother to Bruce, which she must follow him and deliver, and she had warned them that it might take some time: 'He'll probably want to ask me dozens of questions – he's got no idea about gardening, I have to tell him everything.' But they'd never believe she'd been answering questions all this while.

Somebody who was still at the swings was Stephen Waddilove. He'd arrived there just before she'd left for the allotment, and appeared no happier now than he had then. Feeling rather sorry for him, she said hallo.

'Hallo,' he said. 'You've come out.'

Sometimes he seemed quite retarded. 'I've been out ages; I'm going home now.'

'You've come out of the shed.'

'What!' said Deena, staggered.

'I saw you go in.'

'Yes that's right, I was down there helping Bruce, we were very busy gardening,' gabbled Deena at top speed.

Stephen followed as she moved away from the swings. 'Was Bruce in the shed too?'

'How do *I* know?' said Deena, beginning to recover. 'I don't know when you were looking. Of course he goes in the shed sometimes, that's what it's for – to keep things in, gardening things. Goodbye, I've got to rush.' She began running. Really, she thought, Stephen was an absolute menace. Why on earth couldn't he play with the other six-year-olds instead of spying on people twice his age?

When she got home her mother knew she'd been at the allotment (Marian had told Linda) and asked if she'd brought the watering can.

'I never thought of it.' She'd never even noticed it.

'And you've been down there all this while – what on earth were you doing, to forget it?'

'Oh I don't know; this and that.'

Her mother rushed on to her next topic (the rubbish under Deena's bed); thank goodness she was usually too busy to listen to the answers to her own questions.

9

When Bruce got home from school the following day he found an unwelcome surprise standing outside the back door. It was the old chair. It looked even more dilapidated in these surroundings than it had in the shed, and Bruce gazed at it in astonishment and exasperation until he saw his mother watching him through the kitchen window.

'Oh, *Mum*,' he said, opening the door.

'Yes, I went and fetched it myself.' She was rather pink. 'You were obviously never going to do it.'

'I didn't know you wanted it that much. It must have taken you ages.'

'Not really. A very kind man gave me a hand part of the way.'

So long as it wasn't anyone who knew them, and would wonder disapprovingly what sort of son allowed his mother to lug great awkward pieces of furniture round the streets.

'How did you get on in your French test?' she asked.

Startled by the sudden question, Bruce told the plain truth. 'Not very well.'

'There you are, I knew it wasn't a good place to study.'

He swore inwardly at the ease with which he had allowed her to prove her point. Not content with taking his chair, did she have to show that he would be better off without it?

'I can still work down there. I don't have to have a chair.'

'Any work you do down there ought to be on the allotment. I was surprised how neglected it looked – I thought you'd been spending so much time on it!'

'Neglected?' said Bruce defensively.

'Covered in weeds.'

'They're only little.' He was rather hurt, he found.

'All the more reason to get them out now, before they grow. I thought you *had* weeded it – I'm sure you told me you had.'

'Well, they grow so fast,' he muttered.

'If we can't take care of it we ought to give it up.'

'Don't let's do that!' He was surprised how little he fancied the idea. The allotment was his place now – which made his mother's intrusion all the more annoying. Perhaps she didn't like him having a place of his own. She certainly hadn't seemed to like the discovery that his father had used it as a retreat. He wondered anxiously how long it would take for her to think of removing the shed.

Deciding to change the subject, he asked: 'Mum, you know Dad's drawing books?'

'His what?' she said blankly.

'You know, those books he used to do his sketching in?'

'Oh yes . . .'

'Where are they?'

She was taken aback. 'What on earth put those into your head?'

'Nothing,' he said impatiently. 'I mean they were in it already. I've been thinking I'd like to look at them. Can I?'

'Well . . .' she said. 'Yes; I suppose you can some time. I don't know exactly where they are, though; with all that stuff I put in the loft, probably.'

'Could I see if I could find them?'

'Oh no, Bruce, I don't want you rooting about up there. I'll have a look for them one day. There's no hurry, is there?'

'I suppose not.'

103

Over tea his mother began talking about the chair again. 'The man who helped me has the allotment next to ours,' she said chattily.

'Does he?'

'Quite elderly, with white hair and a rosy complexion.'

'Mm.'

'You haven't noticed him? When I described you he recognised you immediately.'

'Well, there are lots of old men down there – I can't tell one from another.'

'He says he's often seen you. And Deena, too; at least it sounded like Deena.'

'It would be,' sighed Bruce.

'He said you seem to spend an awful lot of time inside the shed.' A challenging note had crept into his mother's voice. It was particularly noticeable as she added: 'Together.'

Bruce swallowed a large piece of tomato whole.

'Is that right?' she asked.

'No. Of course not.' He was blushing, curse it!

'But I'm sure he wouldn't have made it up.'

'I bet he would, the old goat.'

'Bruce, that's no way to describe anyone! Besides, I thought you didn't know who I was talking about?'

'I'm beginning to get a picture of him now.' They had exchanged hallos once or twice. Nothing more; the man had always seemed absorbed in his own work. Who could have guessed he'd have such sharp eyes?

'Was Deena with you when you were supposed to be learning your French yesterday?'

He didn't dare deny it. 'Well, yes – '

'No wonder you did the test badly!'

'It's not my fault she comes,' he complained, goaded. 'Tell *her* if you don't like it. I wish you would!'

'Now Bruce, it isn't fair to try and blame it all on Deena.'

'Well, I don't ask her to come.'

'Whether you do or not you could ask her to go, I suppose?'

'Huh – you and old Ma Reevy wouldn't like that very much, when you've got the idea we're such friends.'

'Bruce!'

'Oh sorry,' he growled.

'You're being silly. You can't possibly think Mrs Reevy or I want you and Deena spending hours together in a shed.'

Getting out of this was going to be difficult. He abandoned the attempt to blame Deena – richly though she deserved it, it wouldn't help. 'It wasn't hours,' he said, 'and it's only been once or twice. We didn't plan it or anything, it just sort of happened.'

'*What* did?'

'Oh, nothing!' Crimson, Bruce wondered which she'd mind most: confirmation of her wordless suspicions, or the truth? She'd get neither from him, that was certain. 'Nothing at *all*. Just talking. Arguing mostly. And you needn't worry, Mum. She won't be going down there again.'

'Well.' His mother examined this statement doubtfully. 'It's not that I minded her helping you . . . I thought that was very nice, only – '

'Yes, but she's not much use,' Bruce put in quickly. 'More of a hindrance than a help actually. Anyway she's bored with it now.'

'Deena always was rather like that.' His mother sounded a bit more contented. 'Volatile.'

Bruce could have thought of other adjectives, but he let the matter rest.

That morning at school Marian greeted Deena with a knowing grin. 'Did you have a nice time yesterday with Brucey?' she asked.

'With Bruce?' Deena made the correction without thinking, unpleasantly surprised at Marian's tone.

'You were down there long enough.'

'I told you he'd probably keep me talking. You shouldn't have waited.'

'Oh we didn't, did we, Pat? Only as long as we wanted to.'

'I was meeting someone,' said Pat placidly.

'But we couldn't help noticing that you never came back.'

Deena wished she knew how long they had stayed at the swings. If she was being teased about a ten-minute period, that was one thing; if there was an hour to account for, it was a different matter.

She said: 'Well, he goes on so – the great stupid lump.'

Marian laughed. 'It's no good, Dee, you can't fool us that way any longer. Of course I knew there was something funny when I came round the other day, and Linda said you'd been so keen to chase after Bruce you'd forgotten all about me.'

Linda had said that, had she, little beast! Doing her very best to stir things up. No wonder Marian had been a bit cool next day.

'That was just Linda, you know what she is. I was sorry I wasn't there – I said so, didn't I, afterwards?'

'Oh it didn't matter. It meant I could go into town with June and look at the shops.' Deena remembered now, Marian had told her all about the expedition; they'd been followed by a large group of boys pestering them to come to a film, but they'd refused. Marian had obviously enjoyed herself. It would have been different the night before, being left alone when Pat had to meet her boy friend. Perhaps that was why Marian was so acid now.

'And I'm sorry about yesterday too. He's such a drag, Bruce.'

'Come off it, Dee,' said Marian. 'You're trying too hard.'

'And *you're* being too clever by half – I do think he's a drag!'

Marian, unimpressed, didn't stay for further talk. Deena

106

quickly summoned some extra good humour and called after her: 'Coming round tonight?'

'Can't,' the answer floated back, followed by something about June.

It was bloody unfair, raged Deena to herself, if she was going to be teased about Bruce – Bruce, of all people. It looked like the end of her easy friendship with Marian. Would it have been any better if she'd invented and confided all kinds of cosy details? No – Marian wouldn't have liked that either. Anyway she couldn't have done it, not about Bruce.

'I often thought he looked rather nice,' said Pat, reminding Deena of her presence. She sounded sympathetic, but Deena wasn't in the mood for that sort of sympathy.

'Then you must be mad,' she snapped, and walked away, not caring how Pat's expression changed. Pat had always been a bit soppy.

Her mood grew steadily worse throughout the day, and she pounced on Linda as soon as she got home.

'What do you mean by telling Marian such a load of rubbish the other evening?'

'I never did!' protested Linda. 'What rubbish?'

'You know. That I'd gone off after Bruce.'

'Well, it was true,' said Linda, injured. 'And it sounded a lot better than what you told me to say, about you'd got fed up waiting.'

Deena did dimly remember giving some such instruction, but recalling it did nothing to soothe her present bad temper.

'Of course it wasn't true!'

'Oh yes it was,' said Linda, retreating quickly towards the kitchen and the safe neighbourhood of her mother. 'You're always going after him, you know you are. Whenever he goes down to his allotment you go too.'

'I go to help with the gardening – so what?'

'Ah ha, no you don't!' crowed Linda. 'You spend all your time shut up inside the shed with him!'

Deena's denial was drowned by Mrs Reevy's eruption into the conversation.

'What on earth are you talking about?' she asked Linda. 'You shouldn't make up stories like that.'

'It isn't a story, it's true. Stephen saw them. He told Angela. You ask Stephen!'

'That little rat,' said Deena, 'I'll wring his neck!'

'Saw them what?' persisted Mrs Reevy.

'Going inside the shed,' said Linda. 'And they stayed there ages. I expect they were *kissing* – ' she broke off and dodged behind her mother as Deena took a wild swipe in her direction.

'That's enough!' said Mrs Reevy.

'She hurt me,' complained Linda.

'She won't do it again.' Mrs Reevy held open the back door. 'Go and play, then you'll be out of harm's way.'

'I don't want to.'

'Never mind that, just get along.'

Still complaining, Linda went. Deena tried to vanish in the other direction, but was prevented.

'I want a word with you,' her mother said.

'*What?*' said Deena, slouching back.

'And take that look off your face.'

'What look?'

'You know perfectly well what look. Now then.' Mrs Reevy leaned her back against the sink and folded her arms. 'Is it true you and Bruce spend all your time down on that allotment inside the shed?'

'Not *all* of it. Of course not.'

'Most of it?' She didn't wait for an answer. 'I thought there was something funny, you staying so long down there. You're not that keen on gardening.'

'And I'm not that keen on Bruce either!'

'Hmmm. What goes on then? Inside this shed?'

It occurred to Deena that she could say, with perfect truth, *We sleep together*. She snorted.

'You'll laugh on the other side of your face in a minute, my girl,' promised her mother.

Deena sobered herself.

'You haven't answered my question.'

'Why don't you ask Bruce?'

'Because I don't want to upset his mother.'

'Ho no,' muttered Deena, 'mustn't upset her ladyship.'

This provoked a lecture on manners, neighbourliness, and the troubles Mrs Payne had had to undergo. 'And you'd better not let me hear you speaking like that again.'

'No. All right. Can I go and do my homework now?'

'Yes – when you've told me what happens inside the shed.'

Deena took a breath and said: 'It's not your business.'

Her mother took a much larger breath. 'It certainly is my business if you're doing anything you shouldn't!'

'We're not.'

She received a searching look. 'Are you sure of that, Deena?'

'*Yes*.' She left the kitchen, noticing with irritation that Theresa had been sitting in the next room throughout the conversation. As she gained the passage she heard her mother say:

'Did you hear what we were talking about? She does worry me sometimes, you know.'

She had mentioned her homework chiefly as an excuse, but as soon as she had calmed down a little she realised she couldn't start it even if she wanted to, because she had left her satchel in the living room. Also she was hungry. She hung about on the stairs until she judged her mother would have finished discussing her with Theresa, and then returned to the kitchen.

'What are you getting now?' asked her mother, whose mood seemed slightly improved – thanks to Theresa?

'A sandwich.'

'I thought you had so much work to do?'

'I can't work with my stomach rumbling.'

'Oh and Deena, what about that watering can?'

'*What* about it?' said Deena uncooperatively.

'When are you going to go and get it back?'

Deena spread a thick layer of pickle on her bread. 'I don't know.'

'Well, how about today? It can't stay down there for ever.'

'Oh, not today – I don't feel like walking all that way today. Besides, Bruce might be there.'

'Well, then you can explain you're taking it. He might wonder what had happened to it otherwise.'

Deena said cunningly: 'He might entice me into the shed again, and keep me there for hours.' She took her sandwich and vanished, holding it with both hands to keep the pickle in. Her mother had time for no more than an exasperated sigh.

'She never does what I ask her to,' she complained to Theresa. 'I wish she was more like Bruce.'

'Well,' said Theresa, 'if she really wants to avoid him you don't have to worry so much about that, do you?'

'What about my watering can, though?'

Theresa looked at her homework, thought there was little prospect of getting it done while her mother was in such an anxious and talkative mood, and said: 'Oh, I'll get it.'

'But it ought to be Deena, not you.'

'You'll never make her go without a scene.'

'You're right.' Mrs Reevy ran a hand through her hair. 'I don't know what it is about her – she's more trouble than the rest of you put together!'

'Mm.' Theresa closed her books and piled them up. 'I won't be long.'

She decided she had better check first that the watering can actually was still down at the allotment. Crossing the road, she knocked at the door and explained her errand to Mrs Payne, who called Bruce to deal with it.

'Yes, it is still down there – I think,' he said.

'He'll get it for you. Don't you bother to go,' said his mother.

'No, it's all right, I don't mind. You're in the middle of your tea, aren't you?'

Bruce said he had finished. A little more polite skirmishing resulted in both of them setting off together for the allotment.

They walked in silence at first. Theresa, searching for possible subjects of conversation, asked Bruce if he knew what he wanted to do when he left school.

'Not really,' he said. 'You want to be a teacher, don't you?'

'Yes.'

'You'll be good at it, I expect.'

'I worry sometimes about whether I'll be able to make them behave themselves.'

'Oh, I should think that would be easy; when you're wearing a habit, just the look of you will make them pay attention.'

'I don't intend to be a nun,' protested Theresa, blushing slightly.

'I am sorry.' Bruce blushed too. 'I know you don't really, of course – it's because you always remind me of Sister Pauline, at St Joseph's.'

'Oh,' said Theresa.

'Nicely, I mean! You don't mind, do you? I always liked her. She was my favourite teacher.'

Theresa smiled and admitted: 'I liked her too. If I ever teach half that well I'll be jolly pleased.'

They reached the allotment.

'Now I *hope* the watering can's in the shed.' Bruce opened the door and groaned.

'What? Isn't it there?'

'Oh yes – it's just the shed looks so bare. I'd forgotten about Mum taking the armchair away.'

'The armchair?'

'It was an awful old wicker thing that Dad kept down here. It was quite comfortable though, and I'd got used to having it – but Mum didn't like it being here.'

'Didn't she want you and Deena to use the shed as a den?'

'A *den* – we're much too old for dens. Anyway, how did you . . .'

'Stephen Waddilove noticed, apparently, that you were often in here together. Mum was a bit bothered.'

'About us having a den?' said Bruce with a touch of sarcasm.

'I told her I thought that was all it was.'

'And what did Deena say?'

'Nothing. She made rather a mystery of it; which did nothing to soothe Mum, of course. Bruce, I don't know what you've been up to, but do you think you ought to stop?'

'Have you told Deena to stop?'

'Dee doesn't do what I tell her – but anyway I think maybe it's more up to you.'

'Oh do you!' said Bruce. 'Before, you were afraid she was leading me astray.'

'I know. I've changed my mind.'

'Why?'

Theresa said slowly: 'I suppose, because she seems not very happy; as though she's in a situation she doesn't like.'

'That's *her* fault. It is, really. Like I told my mother – I don't ask her to come down here. I wish people would believe me.'

'Well,' said Theresa, sounding half convinced, 'all right. Here, give me the watering can; I must be getting back.'

10

'I suppose I'd better go and get that watering can,' said Deena the following evening.

'Oh, it's all right, it's been got,' said Theresa.

'Got! Who by?'

'Me.'

Deena was surprised to find that she was annoyed. The fetching of the can had been in her head as an irritating chore to be performed; but now it no longer needed doing she felt quite bereft.

'When did you?' she asked.

'Yesterday evening, just after you'd said you wouldn't.'

'*Why?* It wasn't that urgent.'

'I don't know; I suppose I felt like the walk.'

After a moment Deena said: 'Was Bruce down there?'

'He came down with me. I went to their house first.'

'But you didn't *both* need to go!'

'Well,' said Theresa mildly, 'we both wanted to, I suppose.'

'Huh. I bet his mother made him.'

'Yes, I think it was her idea.'

Deena both wanted and dreaded to know more. She said: 'Did you talk?'

'A bit. We couldn't go all that way in silence.'

'Bruce could,' snorted Deena.

'Well, he didn't.'

'What did you talk about?'

'I'm not sure I can remember.'

She sounded cagey, Deena thought. 'Me?'

Theresa said: 'Why should we talk about you?'

'*Did* you, that's the point,' snarled Deena.

'Not really. Only about you and Bruce liking the shed.'

'Liking it!' said Deena scornfully. 'Did Bruce say I liked it?'

Theresa looked uncertain. 'Well, not in so many words. He said you kept going there.'

Although it was true, the knowledge that Bruce had said this to Theresa made Deena so outraged and humiliated she was unable to speak.

'Dee . . .' said Theresa hesitantly, 'if you don't like going, I shouldn't if I were you. That was partly why I fetched the watering can – so you wouldn't have to go down there if you didn't want to.'

'I wish you'd keep *out* of my affairs!' Deena could feel tears in her eyes; she rushed upstairs before they had a chance to fall.

He said you kept going there. What else had Bruce said? That she made a nuisance of herself? Oh the beast, the horrible beast. He would never have offered to walk down to the allotment with *her* – she would never have got inside his precious shed at all if she'd waited to be invited. But who wanted to go inside it anyway? How ridiculous to feel jealous of Theresa, how *stupid*!

Gazing unseeingly through her bedroom window, she was brought abruptly to attention when the object of her thoughts came out of his house opposite and turned down the street. He must be going to the allotment. If Theresa hadn't been so jolly officious the day before, appropriating other people's jobs so freely, she'd have met him down there. She would have walked past coldly without a word – or perhaps she'd have brandished the watering can and said something cutting about those who didn't bother to return what they'd borrowed. Not that he had borrowed it really, not the second time. She had taken it down there without asking whether he needed it.

She wished she hadn't announced her intention of going to fetch it back; if Theresa hadn't put her right she'd have gone anyway, and would at least have had an encounter with Bruce. Then she realised she could still go; how was Bruce to know that she knew the can had already been fetched? She left the house hurriedly, this time not telling anyone her destination.

As she walked she rehearsed inside her head the sharp remarks she wanted to make to Bruce. If he expected her to keep the secret of the seeds, she would say, he shouldn't go in for nasty conversations about her with her sister. Oh no, that wouldn't do – she wasn't supposed to know about Theresa. Well, she would just ask point-blank *did* he expect her to keep his secret; and leave it to him to see that in that case he owed her rather more conciliatory behaviour.

The allotment was apparently deserted. She felt unusually nervous at the prospect of venturing inside the shed, and made sure she knew exactly what she was going to say. *I've come for the watering can.*

But it was unnecessary; her whole collection of prepared sentences was made redundant by the fact that Bruce was asleep.

Of course, he would be! Why hadn't she expected it? And why was he sitting on the floor – where was his chair? He hadn't provided himself with any cushioning; he would, she thought with satisfaction, be very sore when he woke.

He hadn't been very careful with the seeds this time. She could see some on the floor beside him. He must have taken her at her word when she said she'd had enough of them. It would seem logical to him, no doubt; he had her nicely locked up in his tower, why should she want to dream about that?

Why indeed, she asked herself wryly. Because she was finding she did want to. Maybe his unbearable air of smugness had something to do with it. There he was in his dream world, secure against interference – well, if she couldn't alter that at least she could make him aware of her presence. She was fairly sure that if she entered the dream he would find himself visiting the room where she was imprisoned; and if she didn't, he wouldn't.

She settled down on the floor beside him and helped herself to a seed. She suddenly wondered what would happen if she ate it. He had only looked at his; if she ate one, mightn't that give her an advantage?

She licked it gently, then let it rest on her tongue. There was no taste. Perhaps she was doing something mad. But he was in so much the stronger position – what else could she try? She crunched the seed firmly between her teeth.

It tasted all right. Quite nice, really. Wondering whether to risk any more, she thoughtfully eyed another; then, as the stripes began to wobble, she attempted to look away, but was too late.

The girl stood at the window looking out. Somewhere beyond those softly waving treetops was the sea; but she wasn't high enough for it to be visible. No hope of signalling to any passing ship. On the other hand she was far too high to have any chance of climbing down to the ground.

She didn't know what the boy intended to do with her. He wouldn't say. When he brought her food he refused to linger long enough to answer any questions; he wouldn't even unlock the door unless she called to him first from the other side of the room, so he could tell she wasn't lying in wait to attack him as he came in.

She had been here three days. Her ankle was quite recovered, and the anxiety and boredom were making her desperate. Laid out on the window-sill were the useless contents of her pockets – useless as far as making an escape went, anyway; they were some good as toys. If only she had her knife!

She began to play a game she'd invented with the handful of seeds she had gathered on the morning the boy caught her. Perhaps she should have eaten them; maybe he'd have left her alone if he hadn't found her going after another rabbit.

She could try them now – she felt quite hungry, and he wouldn't be bringing her supper for some time yet. She put one in her mouth and crunched it up. It had an interesting taste; however, she decided she'd better see if there were any ill effects before eating any more.

The waiting made her nervous, and she began to wish she hadn't swallowed it after all. Her heart was beating faster; she was thirsty, and the room seemed very hot. She drank some water and told herself not to imagine things. Then she opened one window wide, kneeling on the sill to get the full benefit of the air, and gazing down at the ground.

It didn't seem so far away as it had earlier. The grass looked smooth and soft. Surely if she hung by her arms and then let herself drop she would land in one piece . . . she turned round and slid over the sill on her stomach, feet first; dangled for a moment with her face to the outside wall of the tower, and let go.

She floated downwards. Of course the air on the island was rather thick. The ground pushed up under her feet, the springy grass acting like a cushion. She waved her arms and managed to keep her balance. She was out of the tower!

She began to run towards the end of the island. She was very light and fast on her feet; the trees went by in a blur. Then she reached the open ground, and soon came to the place where the boy had thrown the stone. There was her knife. So after all he had left it lying out here to be ruined by the weather, although he had said he would pick it up! She would make him sorry he'd been so forgetful.

She returned to the tower at top speed. Knife in hand she swiftly and silently ascended the spiral staircase. A sixth sense told her which room he was in. She burst through the door; he looked at her and froze with incredulous horror. Before he could move from his chair she had crossed the room and was facing him across the table, well within striking distance. He made one feeble effort to rise, but subsided at a menacing wave of the knife.

'Stay where you are,' she hissed, 'and listen to me!'

'How – how – how did you get out?'

'Through the window, of course.'

'That's impossible – you could never have landed safely.'

'My limbs are supple, and I know how to use them. Would you like a demonstration?'

'No,' he croaked, his eyes fixed fearfully on the tip of the blade.

She laughed. 'Don't worry. I won't hurt you if you do as you're told.'

'What do you want me to do?'

'Get me safely off this island. Somehow or other.'

'All right,' said the boy. 'You can take my helicopter. It's on the top of the tower.'

'Show me.'

They went to the top of the tower and there it was. She climbed inside. The controls presented no problem, being exactly the same as those on her speedboat. In a moment she was airborne and heading towards Eldin. She left the island behind and flew high above the sea.

Then the helicopter began to drop. It was out of her control. It fell faster and faster, and she saw the waves come to meet her and closed her eyes, and opened them a moment later to see that she was back in the tower, in the room where she had been for the last three days. She was lying on the bed. When she tried to sit up she couldn't. All that happened was that the boy's face appeared above hers. He was bending over her, frowning.

'Was I in a helicopter?' she asked.

'A helicopter?' he said.

'Have you got one?'

He shook his head. 'You're ill,' he said.

'Yes,' she agreed, laughing. 'Being shut up has made me ill. I may die of it.'

The boy said that would never do. He said he would give her wings to fly away; he fixed them behind her shoulders and launched her through the window and she soared up over the treetops, but she went too high, she was sucked up towards the sun and closed her eyes against its glare and opened them on the tower room and the anxious face of the boy.

Then she made another escape, and another; they went on and on. She no longer laughed in between, but cried in a dreadful weariness. He tried to give her water to drink; it ran over her face and soaked the pillow.

At last it came to an end. She was herself again.

'You were very bad,' said the boy. 'I was worried about you.'

'I'm better now, I think. Only sleepy.'

'Sleep, then. Maybe when you wake you'll want to eat.'

The girl closed her eyes; and Deena woke.

'Thank God that's over,' she said weakly. 'Ugh. What a ghastly experience.'

Bruce was already awake and looking at her. 'Are you all right?'

'I think so. A bit thirsty, that's all.' She tried to swallow, and made a face.

'I don't suppose it's drinking water in the tap down here.'

'Maybe not.'

He felt in his pocket. 'Would a sweet be any good?'

'Oh yes. Thanks.' She unwrapped it eagerly.

'I wonder why it happened?'

She sucked the sweet and didn't reply until the fruity flavour had quite banished the unpleasant taste in her mouth. 'Yes,' she said then, having decided not to tell the truth. 'I wonder.'

Her sufferings must have impressed him, she thought. At any rate he hadn't started ranting at her for being here again in the shed; which was just as well, because she didn't think she could deal with it at the moment. She didn't even want to try standing up yet; she needed a few more minutes of sitting quietly first.

He said: 'Was it . . . as frightening as it looked?'

'Not frightening exactly. Just horrible. Enough to put me right off.'

'I did think the last time might have done that,' he murmured with unusual mildness.

She made a slightly self-conscious face. 'Yes, well.'

There was a short silence which neither found easy to break, and which was ended by a faint sound at the door. Before their suddenly alarmed eyes the handle turned slowly, first one way and then the other.

'The man whose allotment's next door – ' he breathed. 'He *watches* – he told my mother about you – '

Deena was struggling up from the floor. He gave her a hand. 'Stephen,' she began, naming the source from which her own mother's information had come; then as the door opened she said on a different note: 'Stephen!'

'Hallo,' he said, coming inside.

'What on *earth* are you doing here?' It crossed her mind that he might have been sent with a message, and she looked anxiously at her watch; the dream had taken even longer than usual.

'I want to be in your game. Can I?'

'What game?' asked Bruce.

'The game you play in here. Can I be in it?' He added earnestly: 'I'll do what you tell me.'

'What we tell you is to go away and stay away!' snapped Deena. 'We don't want you hanging about – all right?'

'My shed's a bit small for three,' said Bruce. 'And I don't actually have a game.' By his slight emphasis on *my* and *I*, and his reasonable tone, Bruce managed to convey that he thought Deena had spoken out of turn and too harshly. She, paying no attention, carried on:

'And don't go telling any more stories to Angela or Linda or anybody about us coming down here. It's none of your business what we do!'

'But I'd like to play,' persisted Stephen with the awful doggedness of which only he was capable. 'I want to. Why can't I?'

'Listen.' Bruce bent towards him. 'I don't play; I'm too old. I come in here for a bit of peace. And *sometimes* I let Deena come in too, because she's as old as me and she knows how to keep quiet. But it isn't a place for little children; they'd only get bored.'

'I know how to keep quiet,' said Stephen. 'I could go to sleep too.' Abruptly, like someone shamming dead, he slumped on to the floor, dropped his head sideways and snored. 'See?' he said, opening his eyes. 'I could go to sleep just like you.'

'You've been peeping through the window!' accused Deena.

Bruce's voice overrode hers. 'Nonsense, of course we don't go to sleep. We just sit quietly and think.'

Deena thought he didn't realise the danger they were in. What Stephen had just mimed could well have been one of them not merely sleeping, but in the act of falling asleep – and if he had seen that, did he know about the seeds? She glanced round apprehensively, but there were none in sight; Bruce must have gathered them as soon as he woke.

'What else did you see, you sneaky little spy?' she asked in a threatening voice.

Stephen's eyes slid from her to Bruce. 'Nothing.'

'Of course not, there was nothing to see. Now look,' Bruce was rummaging in his pockets, and she feared that at any moment he would spill seeds all over the floor, 'you take this sweet, and go away. All right?'

Stephen reached very slowly for it. As soon as it was in his hand Bruce held the door open and said: 'Goodbye.'

'Bye,' said Stephen, and ambled off unwrapping the sweet as he went.

'He'll trample your seedlings if he doesn't look where he's going,' said Deena sourly.

'Oh, never mind.' Bruce closed the door. 'Why did you go on at him like that? There was no need.'

'But the little wretch keeps spying on us!'

'He's a pest, I know, but the way you were behaving he'll get the idea there's something worth spying *on*.'

'He already has, if you ask me – and if you think bribing him with sweets will work, you're mad.' Deena's indignation grew as she spoke. 'He'll keep coming back for more.'

'I wasn't bribing him,' said Bruce impatiently. 'I was trying to smooth over your unpleasantness, and it wasn't at all easy. I had to use what I'd got.'

'Yes and what you said was *take this sweet and go away*. If you can't see that's bribery you're off your head.'

There was a short angry silence. Then Bruce said, 'Anyway, *you'd* better go away now. You've been here ages – I bet the man next door has noticed. Did he see you come in?'

'I don't know,' said Deena uncertainly. 'I didn't notice him.'

'If you get in such a flap about a little boy spying I'd have thought you ought to notice a man twenty yards away.'

'Yes – well, so would I, so I reckon he can't have been there.' Her voice grew firmer at his attack. 'Next door which way?'

Bruce pointed to the windowless wall of the shed.

'I'll peep,' said Deena, adding maliciously: 'If he is there we'll both have to stay, I suppose, until he's gone.'

However, when she craned her head carefully round the door there was nobody working on any of the nearer allotments. 'All clear,' she said, and went away quickly before he could produce any more critical remarks about her treatment of Stephen.

11

Bruce was trying to do his homework. He couldn't concentrate properly because he kept thinking about the island; in particular remembering the most recent dream, now three days old. It had frightened him a little. Deena had looked quite flattened when she woke, almost as exhausted as the girl in the dream when she'd recovered from her strange delirium. He thought there might be something freakish about the seeds; maybe next time he stared at them it would happen to him. But he didn't want never to use them again. The island drew him, even with the complication of the imprisoned girl.

He sighed. It seemed a long while since he had last been there. He looked despairingly at the blank page in front of him; all he'd done so far was two lines. It was stupid – he couldn't write his essay because he was thinking about the island, and he couldn't go down to the allotment because he had his essay to write.

'You look tired,' said his mother. 'Maybe you should have an early night.'

Bruce came to a sudden decision and put down his pen.

'What I need at the moment is some fresh air.'

'You're not going out now, are you? Where?'

'Oh – just for a walk.'

'Not to the allotment, I hope!'

'I might.'

'I don't like you spending all your time down there. Last

Friday you were away hours. You'll be in that shed I suppose – I don't know how you can.'

'What, after you did your best to make it uncomfortable, you mean?' said Bruce bitterly.

His mother evaded this. 'I've been thinking; maybe we ought to give the allotment up. You don't seem to have a knack for gardening any more than your father had.'

'But if we give it up now all my work will be wasted!'

'Well, I don't know . . . how much work have you actually done? Maybe you did to begin with, but it's something else that takes you down there now, and I don't like it.'

'What you don't like is me having any privacy!' Suddenly he didn't care what he said. 'You can't bear the idea of me having a place where I go for a bit of peace, any more than you could when Dad was doing it!'

'Bruce . . .'

'You can't keep me at home *all* the while. If you get rid of the allotment I'll go somewhere else, that's all!'

He didn't stay for an answer. His mother's face was ominously flushed and he had a feeling she might be about to cry. If she did the embarrassment would be unbearable. He rushed up to his bedroom, snatched the tin of seeds from the drawer, and fled from the house.

Stephen was at the swings. 'Hallo,' he said to Bruce. 'Are you going down to your shed?'

'To the allotment, yes.'

Stephen didn't ask if he could come too, which proved to Bruce that his handling of him the other day had been right, whatever Deena said. Just to make things quite clear he said quickly: 'I'm afraid I haven't got any sweets today.'

'Oh,' said Stephen.

Bruce hurried on. He could hardly wait to reach the shed and lose himself in sleep; it was the only way he could stop himself remembering what he had said to his mother and how she had looked.

He wondered if Deena would join him today. He found to his surprise that he didn't really mind the possibility. He wanted the boy to get a move on and resolve the awkward situation in the tower, and he couldn't do that unless the girl took part in the dream. Of course most people wouldn't have dared try the seeds again after an experience like Deena's, but somehow he didn't see her being permanently put off. He would make sure she could find them; having taken out a couple to use he left the tin in plain view on the floor beside him.

The boy was preparing food for himself and the girl. Originally it had been just for her, but the sight of it reminded him he was hungry. He wanted to talk to her, so he thought they might as well eat together during the discussion. He didn't feel at all uneasy about doing this; she had been much more docile since her strange illness – or perhaps it was just that he saw her differently since he'd had to nurse her through it.

He carried the tray up to her room. She was standing by the window, and her face brightened as he came in.

'I've been wanting to talk to you,' she said eagerly.

'That's funny; I've got something to tell you too. Come and eat.'

She joined him on the bed, but was too full of what she had to say to pay much attention to the food.

'Listen,' she began, 'about your carvings, first . . .'

He felt his face stiffen. He had not been inside his work-room since the dreadful day when he'd first seen the damage she had done there.

'I'm sorry I broke them. I should have told you before. I was sorry almost as soon as I'd done it, actually. I was so upset over my boat –'

'Oh yes, your boat –' he began.

'It doesn't matter,' she said. 'I expect you were in a temper too, at the time. The thing is, it's done. I haven't got a boat any more. I can never get away from here. So please, if I've got to live here for ever, may I live free? I'll do everything your way; I'll never kill any of the animals again. But please, can't we be ... friends?'

She was so determined to speak he had to let her finish. As soon as she stopped he said quickly: 'There's no need.'

A chill came over her face. 'No need?'

'Not for any of that. I was going to say, about your boat – I misled you. I wish I hadn't.'

She stared.

'It's hidden,' he said. 'It isn't destroyed. It's quite safe.'

She looked round her prison. 'Then *why* ...'

'I shut you up to give myself time to think. It was hard at first to see what to do. I didn't want to let you go away because you know the way here; as long as that's true, I can never feel really secure. But now I know how to do it. There are berries on the island that make people forget; you must eat some just before you go, and then all this will vanish from your memory. You'll be free, and I'll be safe.'

He ended on a triumphant note. Then he saw that her face was full of doubt and panic.

'I won't eat anything like that,' she said.

'There's nothing to be afraid of. All they'll do is make you forget the last few weeks. They take about an hour to act, which gives you time to get well away.'

'But I wouldn't be back to Eldin by then. I'd need at least eighty minutes.'

'Oh well – you'll be much more than halfway. It'll be in view, you'll have no difficulty.'

'Suppose it isn't? Suppose anything sends me off course during the hour? Or suppose the berries confuse me so that I can't control the boat?'

'They won't, they'll just make you forget. Anyway, nearer to Eldin won't there be boats looking for you? They'll find you if anything goes wrong.'

She said flatly: 'You can't send me. I won't go. I won't risk dying of thirst adrift in my boat like that.'

'But the risk is so slight!' he exclaimed in exasperation. 'Isn't it worth it to be free?'

'Why can't you let me go free properly? Please!' she begged. 'I promise I'll never tell anyone about your island. And I'll never come back – if you'd rather I didn't,' she added softly.

'How could I believe you?' he said, ignoring her last few words.

'You could, that's all. I *promise*.'

He put his head in his hands and groaned. 'We'll have to talk more about it later. Eat your food now.'

She reached for some, then put it down. 'I don't want any.'

'Why not?' He guessed. 'You don't imagine I've put the berries in it already, do you? Because I haven't.'

'I'm just not hungry.'

He looked at her for a moment and then said: 'I don't know how you suppose we'd have a chance of existing together peacefully, if neither of us trusts the other.'

Her face twitched, but she didn't speak.

'I'll leave the food. You might want it later.'

He went out. She had managed once again to throw his thoughts into chaos, and he needed some time alone to get them straight. A walk by the sea might help.

Deena's mother caught her just as she was sliding out of the house.

'And where are you off to?' she asked grimly.

'Out for a bit, that's all.'

'I suppose you mean another two hours down in that shed.'

'No! I'll be back long before two hours.'

'Deena, I don't like it. If you want to spend time with Bruce why can't you ask him round here, or go round there . . .' (Deena's expression became so mutinous her mother couldn't fail to notice) '. . . or at least go to the Youth Club with him, or something normal! Why have you got to be different from everyone else?'

'Why not?'

'If you keep on like this I shall have to ask your father to have a word with you.'

'Okay,' said Deena indifferently.

'And I'd better have a word with Mrs Payne myself.'

'Oh God no, Mum, don't do that!'

Somewhat surprised at the reaction she'd produced, Mrs Reevy was nevertheless quick to make use of it. 'Well, you give me no option, carrying on the way you do.'

'I'm not carrying on any way, honestly I'm not. I just feel like going out for a bit now, and I suppose I might talk to Bruce if I see him, but I won't be gone long – nothing like two hours, really.'

'Well, you see you're not. Otherwise I will have to talk to her; I mean it, Deena.'

'I know you do,' muttered Deena, 'worse luck.'

'What did you say?'

'Nothing. Bye!'

She ran down the street, trying by physical exertion to smother the awful inner cringing she felt at the thought of herself and Bruce being discussed by their two mothers. Perhaps she ought not to go to the allotment at all – or ought she to warn him of what might be going to happen, and maybe apologise? This must be the last time, though. She'd said that before, but it really must.

As she passed the swings Stephen called out: 'Bruce is in the shed.' Deena tossed her hair back and pretended not to hear.

She wouldn't be able to talk to Bruce, then; or at least not until he woke. So she might as well dream herself – one last short dream before she rushed back home to placate her mother.

Virtuously she checked the next door allotment and was glad to see the inquisitive old man wasn't there. Inside the shed she took a seed from Bruce's lap and sat down, wondering as she did so what the small tin in the middle of the floor was for, but not wanting to spare any time to examine it. Because she had to be quick she held the seed at arm's length, and peered; although the wavering of the stripes was only just visible, it was enough.

After the boy had gone out she was too disturbed to sit still. She paced up and down the room and tried to make plans, but her brain would only produce, alternately, a picture first of her miraculously undamaged boat hidden somewhere on the island, and second of her in the boat, lost at sea, crazed from the effects of the berries and having run out of food and water.

Hunger made her pause for a moment beside the bed and eye the contents of the tray. When she remembered that the boy had been eating while he talked she risked a few bites herself, though she was too anxious to enjoy it. Munching a red fruit she went towards the window; then stood still in amazement, looking out.

Down below somebody had come into the clearing. It was a child; a small fat boy in a pair of swimming trunks and nothing else. He was walking in an odd way, very slowly and drunkenly, and as she watched he took something from the cupped palm of one hand and put it into his mouth. Then his legs gave out. He wobbled downwards into a sitting position, made a few slow chewing movements with his mouth, and fell sideways until his cheek touched the grass.

The girl shouted to him from the window but he didn't stir. She ran across the room, shouting now for the older boy; she banged on the door, rattled the handle, turned it – and found to her astonishment that she could get out. The boy must have forgotten to turn the key when he left.

When she reached the bottom of the tower the child was whimpering and struggling to rise. She knelt beside him and half lifted him into her arms; he was heavy and awkward, resisting her at first and then clinging to her with a frantic grip as he cried, 'Mummy, Mummy! The shark! The shark!'

'It's all right,' she soothed. 'There is no shark, you're safe, there's no shark here.'

'No shark . . .' he echoed, and relaxed a little. 'No shark . . . no shark . . . no shark . . .'

'You were eating something,' she said, looking at his empty hands. 'What were you eating?'

'No shark . . .' he said in a drowsy monotone. 'No shark . . .'

She explored the grass with her fingertips, half knowing what she would find, but horrified none the less when she came upon the small striped seeds. He must have gathered them in the wood; they were exactly the same as hers upstairs. She gave him a little shake and held one before his eyes.

'How many?' she asked. 'How many did you eat?'

He stared and then screamed, 'Tooth! Don't bite me, don't bite me!'

She dropped the seed and began soothing him again. He seemed to fall asleep; she held him as still as she could, her thighs aching under his weight, until the boy came into the clearing.

The boy was carrying an extraordinary object – extraordinary, at least, in this setting. It was a large inflated rubber duck, bright blue, with a yellow beak. It was big enough for a child to sit astride, and the girl guessed at once that that was what had brought the child in her arms to the island.

The boy, seeing the two of them together, looked much too astounded to make any deductions at all.

'You – what's happening?' he said. 'Who's he?'

'Sssh. I don't know,' she whispered. 'I saw him from the window, and came down – oh, you'd forgotten to lock the door – '

Her caution was in vain; the child opened his eyes, saw the boy and the duck, and began to scream again.

'No! Don't let it eat me, don't let it, don't let it!'

'Hush, hush, it won't eat you, you're quite safe. – Go *away*,' she added in a fierce aside. '*Hide* that thing.'

'I don't understand,' said the boy, putting the duck inside the door of the tower and then returning to stand discreetly behind and a little distant from the child.

'He's ill,' said the girl. 'He's eaten some seeds . . . there, hush, go to sleep; Mummy's got you.'

The boy made an incredulous face.

'That's who he thinks I am – at least, he did at first.' The child's head lolled; he started to snore. 'Look, he ate some of these.'

'They're from the white flowers!'

'Yes.'

'You had some, didn't you; I saw them when you were ill. You're not meant to *eat* them. I never do.'

'No, well of course you wouldn't if you knew what they did.'

'What?'

'This.' She pointed to the child, adding rather hopelessly, 'Then you *don't* know – you didn't realise, when I was ill, it was because I'd eaten one? Just one – I think he's had more. And you don't know what we should do to make him better?'

He looked baffled. 'I've no idea. Why did you eat one?'

'I was hungry. I expect he was too. Listen, will you help me take him inside and put him to bed? We can at least do that.'

'All right.'

'I'll be able to carry him, if you lift him and give him to

132

me when I'm up. You might have to help me a bit on the stairs. Where's the lowest room with a bed?'

The child made things easier by remaining unconscious during the next ten minutes, but as soon as they had him on a bed he opened his eyes and began screaming and thrashing about. They had to imprison him under a tightly tucked-in sheet to prevent him flinging himself on to the floor. He no longer seemed to find the girl a friendly presence, although she spoke as soothingly as she could. Eventually the seizure passed and he fell asleep again.

'He needs a doctor,' said the girl.

'There isn't one.'

'I know there isn't, *here*. You don't expect to get ill in this paradise of yours, do you? But you see, people can. I did. He has. What would you do if *you* ever did? Stuck here without a boat?'

'Well . . .' he said haltingly, 'there's your boat.'

'There is now.' She was thinking aloud, struggling towards a conclusion so important that she scarcely noticed he had offered her, probably with no strings attached, her longed-for means of escape. She could take the boy to Eldin but there was, wasn't there, some *better* way . . . 'This place is wrong,' she said. 'You living here all alone, everything you need in the storeroom – it's not real.'

'You don't know what you're talking about,' he said angrily.

She exclaimed: 'It's *not* real! It's a dream! And this – this is *Stephen*.'

'No!' said the boy, and as he spoke he was changing, growing thinner, younger, his face . . .

'You're *Bruce*,' she said.

'*Deena!*'

He was furious but she didn't care. She caught hold of him and began to shake him, saying, 'Wake up, you must, we've got to wake up!'

. . . and there was the shed round her, and she really was shaking Bruce, and he was opening his eyes and groaning, 'What? What?'

'Oh look,' said Deena, 'it's *true.*'

The shed had a third occupant. Stephen Waddilove was lying on his back breathing in snorts, his face flushed and an empty tin clasped to his chest. The moment he saw him Bruce became fully awake; it was Stephen's turn to be shaken, then slapped, and shouted at – all to no effect. He was heavily unconscious, and so he remained.

12

'It's too soon,' said Bruce, 'it must be like the time I tried to wake you, and couldn't.'

'When did you?'

'Oh – I forget exactly, but it was one time soon after you'd gone to sleep. The effect's too strong then, you have to wait for it to wear off.'

'Well, we can't wait with Stephen.'

'Can't we?'

'Of course not – he's *eaten* them, not just looked at them! They might be poisonous in large doses. How many has he had, anyway?'

'I think there were about seven in the tin.'

They searched the floor, but found nothing. 'He's had ten, then,' said Bruce; 'there were ten altogether.'

'He would go and gobble the lot. He must have crammed them in like anything; if he'd been interested enough to look what he was eating he'd never have managed them all. And the hospital are going to want to know what he's taken – we'll just have to describe them as best we can, I suppose.'

'Hospital?' said Bruce stupidly.

'That's where he'll have to go. Can you carry him as far as the park entrance? I should think that's the nearest bit of road. I'll run on ahead and ring 999.'

'Why 999?'

'To get an ambulance, of course!' She rushed away.

It was all very well for her to just assume he would do as

he was told, thought Bruce resentfully. He shouldn't have allowed her to escape like that before they'd discussed the alternatives. Though in fact there were no alternatives. Perhaps he'd realised that when he let her go.

He began to struggle with Stephen's sleeping weight. She could at least have helped with the lifting. Eventually he got him slung over one shoulder and stood up.

He set off at a good pace, but slowed to a crawl on the steep path. He was exhausted when the swings came into view and looked hopefully to see who was there. Gone was all desire to keep Stephen's condition secret; he only wanted help. Unfortunately the largest person present was Linda Reevy, who was simply a nuisance, buzzing round him full of eager questions.

'What's happened? Has he fainted? Where was Deena rushing off to just now? Did you and Deena thump him for spying on you?'

'Is he dying?' asked Angela Reevy.

'Shut up,' panted Bruce. 'Here, he's slipping; come on this side and give him a shove.'

It seemed to take half an hour to reach the park gates. He arrived at the same moment as the ambulance.

'Why didn't you come back and help?' he asked Deena, as Stephen was put inside.

'They said I had to wait here until they arrived. I'm going with him – will you tell his mother what's happened?'

'Well all right, I suppose . . .'

She was already climbing into the back. 'And my mother!' she called as the doors closed.

'And *my* mother,' thought Bruce with extreme gloom. The ambulance drove away and he began to walk slowly home. What on earth was he to tell everybody? He and Deena should have agreed on a story. He had better just stick to the bare essentials; Stephen had found some seeds belonging to him, and eaten them. He must try to imply that he and

Deena hadn't been in the shed at the time but had found him later. Stephen wouldn't be able to contradict, not yet, anyway –

He turned suddenly cold with horror, partly because Stephen might never be able to contradict, but more at the realisation that he had, for a brief moment, felt such a result would be convenient. He tried to blot out the memory with a hurried prayer for Stephen's safety. Was it likely the seeds would be poisonous? When the girl had eaten one, she'd recovered completely, but that of course happened in the dream world – or did it? How had Deena recognised, even while dreaming, Stephen's urgent need for help? Could it be because she'd done the same thing herself? What had she said – 'they might be poisonous *in large doses*.' That must be it; she'd eaten one seed, and it had caused her illness in the dream. How could she have been so stupid? *She* wasn't six years old! No wonder she'd kept it secret.

He turned into his own road, again trying to think of words with which to break his news, and saw that it was half broken. Linda and Angela must have rushed ahead and given their garbled version of the facts; on the pavement ahead his mother and Deena's were supporting a distraught Mrs Waddilove. He broke into a run.

The awkward part of his story was easily avoided. What they wanted to know, after he'd explained about the seeds, was where Stephen was now; and he realised to his chagrin that he didn't know to which hospital he had been taken. Mrs Waddilove became hysterical, and his own mother was embarrassed by his lack of forethought, but Mrs Reevy took it all in her stride.

'A couple of phone calls will settle it, and I'll ring for a taxi as well, you can be there in a moment, and while we're waiting I'll make a cup of tea . . .'

'I'll do that,' said Mrs Payne, and Bruce was left alone as Mrs Reevy swept them over the road and into her house. Not seeing much point in following, he went indoors. He felt thirsty himself, but couldn't be bothered to wait while a kettle boiled; he drank some water and then wandered restlessly from room to room until his mother came in.

'It was the City,' she said. 'Mrs Reevy's gone with her.'

'Ah.'

'He's still unconscious, they said. They're using a stomach pump – Bruce, whatever seeds were they? Where did they come from?'

He explained.

'And you were keeping them in the shed?'

'Sometimes they were here, but they were in the shed when Stephen found them, yes.'

'It's a pity you and Deena weren't there.'

Relieved at her assumption, Bruce said: 'Well, we don't spend *all* our time inside the shed, you know, whatever that man may have told you. We do do a bit of weeding, and things.'

'You can't have been paying much attention to what was going on.'

'I expect we were talking – anyway, Stephen can be awfully crafty, the way he sneaks about.' As soon as these words were spoken Bruce regretted them. He said uncomfortably: 'The other children don't play with him much; I suppose that's why he kept hanging round us. I hope he's all right.'

'I'll ring the hospital in a little while. I don't want to pester them too much. – Would you like a cup of coffee?'

'I think I'd better have another go at my essay really.'

'Well, I'll bring one in to you.'

'Thanks,' said Bruce, surprised.

He was glad he had something on which to concentrate – not that his concentration was of a very high order. Still, somehow the essay got written. It was probably the worst bit of work he had ever done, he thought as he started the last paragraph. Then he heard the sound of a telephone number being dialled, and broke off in mid-sentence as he strained his ears unsuccessfully to listen.

His mother came into the room. 'Well, he's conscious,' she said.

'Is he all right?'

'I think so. They're keeping him in for a while for observation, but I gathered there was nothing wrong as far as they could tell.'

'Thank God for that.'

'Bruce . . .' In mid-reproof his mother changed her tone, saying quietly: 'Yes. Thank God.'

'I bet Mrs Waddilove is relieved.'

'She's a widow, you know. She told us while we were waiting for the taxi. She talked more then than she has in the past five years put together. He was killed in a factory accident up North – they'd only been married a couple of years, and by the sound of it she took it terribly hard. She moved down here because she couldn't bear to stay anywhere near the places and people they'd known together. I think she's never really started living again since it happened.' Although Bruce was listening with interest his mother broke off as though embarrassed by her own words, and took refuge in a change of subject. 'Oh, Bruce, you never drank that coffee.'

'Bother, I did mean to. It's cold now. I'll make some more – would you like some?'

'I'll do it.' They both went into the kitchen. 'They said at the hospital how sensible you and Deena had been to get Stephen there so quickly. It was a good thing you kept your heads.'

'Oh well, it was mostly Deena. Though it was me that carried him, I suppose.'

'You acted together, didn't you. Not everyone can cope in a crisis; your father never could.'

Bruce said: 'Well, he was a very gentle sort of person.'

'I know. You needn't defend him like that.'

'I only meant – ' said Bruce awkwardly.

'I know,' said his mother again. 'He *was* a very gentle sort of person. You loved him for that and so did I. And even if it grew into something more . . . into a kind of weakness that crippled him . . . that wasn't his fault. I don't think it'll happen to you.'

'Used you to?' said Bruce, astonished and illuminated.

'It has sometimes worried me a bit. In some ways you're so like him – and I'm afraid I have tried to thwart that part of you; I *didn't* like you wanting to get away by yourself the way you have been lately. But perhaps it was silly of me.'

'Well,' said Bruce guiltily, 'I've been nasty, I know.' It was the nearest he could get to an apology for his words to her before he'd gone out – only a few hours earlier; it seemed weeks away.

'Those drawings of his – I'll get them out for you one day soon. I think I could lay my hands on them at once if I went up in the loft.'

'Oh, it doesn't matter!'

'No, I'd like to see them again myself. I didn't look at anything when I was packing his stuff away, but I think I'd like to now.'

Bruce felt a lightheartedness that he couldn't express. He said: 'The kettle's boiling!'

'I'll make the coffee,' said his mother.

The next day Bruce walked down to the allotment after school. He wasn't sure why he wanted to; except that after he'd told his mother where he was going and she'd accepted it without criticism he thought maybe he'd been testing her to see if she would stand by what she'd said.

When he got there he took a long critical look, and had to agree that it once again possessed a neglected air. The things he had planted were coming up, but they were hard to spot among the weeds; and the rest of the ground was just being wasted. He began to weed the lettuces, thinking he might as well do something useful now he was here.

Once or twice he glanced towards the shed. It was funny that his mother should have become resigned to his spending time there just when he had ceased to have any reason for doing so. Perhaps he would direct all his energy towards the care of the allotment instead. At least he would no longer be bothered by Deena; she would be unlikely to come down here now that the seeds were all gone. He felt a perverse regret at the thought and was quite pleased, when he had got halfway along the lettuces, to have it proved wrong by her appearance.

'Hallo,' she said meekly. 'Can I help?'

'Do you really want to?'

'Yes.'

'All right then.'

It was a serious offer, he found; she applied herself to the job and did it properly. She even worked without talking until he said:

'I wonder how Stephen is today.'

'Oh, he's fine – he's coming home tomorrow morning. The kids are all longing to see him; Linda's organising a welcome committee. He's rather a hero at the moment.'

'Poor old Stephen, that should make a change. He might even think it was worth the nastiness.'

'I doubt it,' said Deena soberly. 'He must have had a horrible time. It was bad enough for me after only one.'

'So you did have one!'

She blushed. 'Yes.'

'You're mad. Why?'

'Oh, I don't know – it seemed worth a try at the time. Everything was so desperate.'

'But you didn't have to keep joining in the dreams if you didn't want to.'

She made no answer to this, saying next: 'Anyway,

Stephen was all right once he woke. It was just like waking from a nightmare – well, that's exactly what it was, I suppose. And he didn't give us away – or if he did nobody paid any attention; I expect it would have sounded like part of the dream.'

'Thank heavens,' said Bruce, relieved. 'How do you know all this?'

'My mother's sort of adopted Stephen's since it happened. She'd have done it long ago if it hadn't been for that funny manner of Mrs Waddilove's, putting everyone off – this gave her her chance. She's going to introduce her to the social club and God knows what.'

'Poor Mrs Waddilove.'

Deena giggled. 'Yes, she's not sure what's hit her. Oh, it might not be such a bad thing, though. I think she was really lonely before.' She pulled one last weed, then straightened herself and eyed the results of their work. 'There.'

'It looks a lot better now,' said Bruce. 'Thanks.'

'Do you want to do the rest?'

'Doesn't seem much point when there's nothing growing in it. I ought to get on and plant some more stuff. I wonder what.'

'Oh, there must be lots of things – I'm sure I could think of tons. Or do you want to have your own ideas?'

'Well, not necessarily.'

'I could go and look at the gardening counter in Woolworth's, or I expect there are catalogues – hey, I suppose you never thought of planting one of those seeds?'

'No,' said Bruce, and was gripped by a dreadful disappointment as he realised what a chance he had missed. 'And it's too late now.'

'I'm sorry,' said Deena.

'What for?'

'If you'd been by yourself it probably wouldn't have happened.' Bruce had never heard her sound so dejected before.

'How do you make that out?'

'Oh well. If I hadn't kept coming here Stephen might never have noticed just you being in the shed. And I knew you didn't like it. It spoiled your island, didn't it – having that girl there.'

Bruce began to frame a reply, but she didn't give him time to make it.

'I bet you never realised why she kept coming back, though. I bet you thought she did it just to be annoying.'

'Didn't she?'

'No. It was because she liked the boy.'

Bruce considered this. 'She didn't behave as though she did.'

'She did, all the same.'

'How do you know?'

'Because . . .' Deena's voice faltered slightly and she looked at the floor. 'Because it was the same with me. I mean – why I kept coming back. Apart from the seeds being fun, I mean.'

'What *do* you mean?'

Deena's face was very red. She gave him a defiant stare and said: 'I like you. I always have. Even when you turned so nasty and stopped being friends . . .'

'I turned nasty!'

'You know you did.'

'You weren't so specially nice yourself.'

'Well anyway,' said Deena miserably, and then stopped. There was a silence which grew until it seemed unbreakable. Deena looked at the ground and Bruce looked at Deena. He was staggered by the change in her. Deena, the bold mocking Deena! Now was his chance to pay her back for the endless annoyance she had caused him in the past; with a few words he could crush her utterly. Though she looked pretty crushed already. She was sorry she'd spoken – and no wonder. She knew she had put herself into his power.

Suddenly he wished she hadn't. He didn't like to see her

so abject. The normal Deena was much better than this.

He said: 'Well, you did add a certain something to the dreams. They might have got a bit dull without the girl.'

She looked at him doubtfully.

'Yes,' he went on, growing animated as he spoke, 'it was fascinating in a way, wondering what would happen next. And I must have half wanted you to join in, or I'd never have made it so easy for you. I mean, I could have put a bolt on the inside of the shed door, couldn't I? But I never even thought of it.'

'I shan't be able to join in any more though.'

'Well, it was getting so awkward anyway – both our parents wanting to know what we did.'

'*Today* we can tell them weeding, and it'll be true,' said Deena with great satisfaction. Their eyes met, and they laughed.

'You're welcome any time for weeding,' said Bruce, 'if you want to come.'

'I might. If we worked at it we could make this allotment really good.'

'Yes. I was thinking that.'

'We could go and buy some seeds tomorrow.'

'Yes, perhaps we could meet after school, and try Brown's . . .'

They left the allotment and began to go home, making plans as they walked.

'It is a nuisance about the dream, though,' said Bruce. 'I wish we could have known what happened. Whether he sent the girl off in the boat, or let her stay, or what.'

'*I* think he let her go,' said Deena, 'but he didn't make her eat the berry dope; he trusted her not to tell anyone else where the island was, and he didn't mind her coming back to see him other times if she wanted.'

'You sound awfully sure.'

'I am. Now.'